TEMPTING SELON

HISSA WARRIOR BOOK 3

DISCLAIMER

This is a work of fiction. Names, characters, businesses, places, events and incidents are either the products of the author's imagination or used in a fictitious manner. Any resemblance to actual persons, living or dead, or actual events is purely coincidental.

All rights reserved:

Translation:

Don't steal the stories I worked so hard on, and occasionally cried over. Don't get upset at the absolutely made-up story lines: this is a romance, so of course it isn't realistic, duh! Don't be petty and hate on it because it isn't not your kink. We've all got different tastes and there's no shame in that.

Copyright: RK Munin, 2021
Cover Illustration: Natasha Snow Designs
Professional Editing: Jenny Slinger, Owl Eye Proofs and Edits
ISBN-13: 978-1-962699-07-5

Warning: Author is dyslexic as hell.

The editing and beta reading team: Mary Alegre, Gary Anderson, Martha Collins, and Lauren Meghoo

Feel free to contact me with questions, requests, or comments:

Author@RK-Munin.com

Want to get some free novellas or find links to my social media? Everything's on my website:

www.RK-Munin.com

And, as with many writers, your reviews on Amazon, Goodreads, and/or Kindle help immeasurably, even if it's just clicking on the stars.

Thank you to all my readers!

CONTENT WARNING

-The FMC has a traumatic backstory that includes sexual assault.
-The FMC is kidnapped, retraumatized, and rescued.
-There are scenes of violence and fighting.

DEDICATION

To: Mindy K – I couldn't ask for a better adventure buddy!

CHAPTER

1

Lara peers cautiously out the window of her room. It's dark outside, and she doesn't see anyone walking around. She eases the window open, then freezes when it makes a faint sound. When she doesn't hear anyone in the house moving, she finishes opening the window. Once it's open, she waits again, but there aren't any footsteps or the sounds of doors opening. No one's awake. The guards assigned to the house are at the front entrance. If she's careful, they shouldn't see her slip out her bedroom window.

She can hear her good friend Deena sleeping fitfully in the next room. She feels guilty for not going over to try and soothe Deena, but she knows after so many years of friendship that Deena wouldn't appreciate the effort.

Her sister, Mara, should be sound asleep. Mara and her husband Tiran had loud and enthusiastic sex earlier. Considering how long they were at it; Lara can only assume they'll sleep soundly until morning.

Right now, Lara just needs to get out of the house for a bit. Get away from Deena's acerbic commentary about everything. Away from her sister's constant concern and worry. Away from Tiran and the way he always seems to be frowning at her and demanding she remain still and calm. He's always worried that she's going to have a panic attack at any moment. Even when she's doing routine tasks like collecting food or walking down the hall to her room, he watches her like a hawk, poised to jump in to 'soothe' her or call for Mara or Deena to deal with her.

She's tired of the house, and as much as she loves everyone inside, she's tired of them too.

She's not a prisoner. The opposite is true. They would all love for her to leave the house and explore Hissa, her new homeworld. But she can't explore alone. Everyone goes with her everywhere.

Even when she argues, they would pick at least one of them to accompany her. And then there are the guards. Always the guards.

The guards aren't there because they're afraid she'll be attacked on Hissa. No, it's because so many want to meet her.

Decades ago, a virulent epidemic killed every female on the planet and half the male population. The Hissa tried all kinds of things in an attempt to produce children without women but have failed in all endeavors so far. Then Mian rescued Halin, and Mara bought Tiran, and everything changed.

The image of strong, domineering Tiran standing naked at a slave auction, glaring and roaring at everyone still makes Lara giggle. No one would bid on him. Then this slim human woman buys him. Everyone must have thought she was insane.

The other Hissa that found a Decanted human woman is Halin, but he wasn't sold into slavery. His ship was attacked by raiders. Mian chased off the raiders and pulled him off his ship just before it exploded. It was a close call.

Mian and Halin end up falling in love.

Mara and Tiran did the same.

Both women turned out to be reproductively compatible with the Hissa males they chose. In fact, Mian is already pregnant. Far off-world, hunting raiders with the Hissa military, she's growing round with child onboard a Hissa battleship.

The appearance of Mian and Mara and the subsequent pregnancy had a profound effect on the Hissa. It turns out that somehow, human scientists got ahold of a lot of different alien DNA and used it to help create the Decanted Children. The alien

DNA made them grow faster, made them stronger, and most importantly for the Hissa, made them able to have children with Hissa men.

Now, not only are the Hissa actively searching out every Decanted child sold into slavery, but they are also pursuing avenues to buy the Decanting technology from the humans.

And, of course, they also have high hopes Lara will find a Hissa male to enter into a Family Pact with.

That's going to be tough, she thinks to herself wryly, *considering I seem to have a panic attack just about every time a male gets too close.*

Even after the Hissa ruling body, the Council, issued a warning to all Hissa to give her a wide berth, men just couldn't seem to help but approach her. They're never violent or unkind, but she can feel their desperation pressing in on her.

Their need, loneliness, and biological push to have children comes off them in waves whenever she's near. Their acute desire for any compatible female overwhelms her and often triggers panic attacks. She hates it. She hates her fear. She hates the panic attacks. She hates that she makes Deena, Mara, and Tiran so anxious for her.

And that's why she's sneaking out of her window in the middle of the night. Avoiding panic attacks means avoiding men. The only way to avoid men on Hissa is to steal away without telling anyone. It's not as if she's running away. She just needs some quiet time alone. Somewhere outside the house.

She eases out the window and easily drops the dozen feet to the ground. Her enhanced genetics make her graceful and strong even though she didn't work out as much as her twin sister. Mara has always been the fighter, while Lara liked to read and tinker with things.

She might not like to fight, but she does enjoy a good run, and she's an exceptional runner due to her genetics. She takes a few steps to let her muscles warm up, then breaks into an easy jog, keeping a brisk pace she can sustain for miles. Her mental map tells her to head to the left, following the tracks of one of the many slow-moving automated communal trams.

The tram lines run like spokes out of the center of Hissa's nearby capital, all eventually converging at the port where cargo shuttles are constantly landing and taking off. Most Hissa work for either the mining industry or the military. Both of Hissa's moons are packed thick with rare minerals, making them a rich species. And their wealth makes them a tasty target.

Every Hissa is expected to train and be battle worthy, even if they aren't in the military. There are so few Hissa left after the Great Death that if another species ever tries to invade, every last Hissa will need to be prepared to pick up arms and defend or engage in some other wartime duty.

Even with all their wealth, the Hissa are a modest people. They care a great deal about balance. Recreation and Work. Art and Science. Progress and Nature. Their planet is a perfect example.

Tropical in nature, the Hissa homeworld is always warm and smells like rich ripe fruit to Lara. They live in harmony with their planet's dense jungle, letting it grow into their cities in such a way that it enhances rather than impedes the lives of the residents. Even if houses are very close to each other, there's a sense of privacy from dense vegetation encouraged to grow between dwellings.

Even in the heart of the city, the vegetation decorates stone walls and fence lines. In her mind's eye, Lara can picture children laughing and playing as they swing from vines and climb trees. When children start being born from the Hissa / human pairings, they will grow up in a paradise. The thought makes her smile as she runs.

One of the trams trundles toward her. Quickly, she ducks behind a cluster of small trees. At this time of night, she's not surprised to see the tram is empty. Its automated system runs no matter how many or few people are on board. Powered by the same geo-thermal systems the Hissa use to power just about everything, the tram requires little maintenance and no fuel. Lara loves riding it, but tonight she wants to run and feel the warm air caressing her skin as she races through the darkness.

Once the empty tram passes, she starts moving again. It's not long until her feet are on pavement instead of dirt, and there are more tall stone buildings instead of small, single-family dwellings. She's sweating and breathing a little heavy but nothing to alarm her. As long as she doesn't have an adrenaline spike, she can run all night.

The shuttles, illumined as they land at the port, act as guiding lights for her. The busy port is calling to her. Most might assume she'd favor more rural areas where there would be fewer people. But what they don't understand is that after a childhood lived indoors and an adulthood spent in space, nature is foreign to her. She craves metal structures and machinery, not wildlife and jungle.

Rounding a large domed building, the tall control tower fills her vision. It stands at the far end of the port, built so high it looms over not only the port but all of the city as well. Access to the tower is strictly limited because of the many delicate machines housed within and on top. The tower organizes and coordinates the constant traffic between Hissa and her two moons. Lara knows she can't get inside the secure tower, but there are vines growing all the way up the side of the building, and they can support her weight.

A movement out of the corner of her eye makes her dive behind a building just as two men step out of a structure across the tracks from her. She watches the two Hissa men as they talk to each other. They are typical of Hissa males, and she takes a moment to study them.

Both are tall, probably around seven to seven and a half feet, which is an average height for a Hissa. They're also quite muscular because it's a point of pride that all Hissa men stay fit in case the homeworld is ever attacked. Their skin is a light green all over except for a blue scale pattern that starts at the point of a V just over their eyes and widens until it's a few inches in width. The blue continues to the back of their head and down the spine until it fades out at the small of their back.

Neither male is close enough for her to see, but both probably have lavender or purple eyes. She knows from experience that the blue scale patterns change color with their emotions. She's seen Tiran's blue scale pattern darken to the point of looking black when he's upset. And turn purple just before he grabs Mara and hauls her giggling to their bedroom.

They don't have much in the way of ears, just little flaps around their ear holes. But their teeth are very notable as they have long canines that can be very intimidating even when they're trying to smile at her. She wishes she could tell the Council to make a law that no Hissa is allowed to smile at her. It's so disconcerting.

Oh, and they have black claw-like fingernails, just to round out their intimidating visage.

Really tall, check. Fangs and claws, check. In desperate need of women, check.

And just to make things awkward, one of the only single breeding compatible females available on the entire planet just happens to be easily terrified by large men, check.

Sighing silently at her idiocy, she watches the men say goodbye to each other and part ways. Once they're out of sight, she starts off again. It's not long until the tower is right in front of her.

With three long running strides, she leaps and lands almost ten feet up the side of the tower. She feels exhilarated and starts to climb, accelerating as she moves upward.

She's lathered in sweat and breathing hard by the time she reaches the top of the tower but feels a triumphant grin spread over her face. From here, she has a clear view of the shuttles landing and taking off. There's almost a 360-degree view of the whole city. She can even see the lights of several small settlements toward the end of the tram lines far in the distance.

Above her, lazily moving across the sky is Diminish, the smaller of Hissa's two moons. If she's here long enough, she'll get to see the much larger Brimming make her way across the night sky.

Settling herself down to watch the night move around her, she enjoys a feeling of peace. The tower hums under her, the machinery inside giving off gentle vibrations that she finds immensely soothing.

A shuttle starts coming in at an odd angle, and she cocks her head with curiosity. It must have developed some issue when it entered the planet's atmosphere because it's listing slightly as it sinks out of sight. Her suspicions are confirmed when she hears it land with a hard thump, making her wince. That can't have been comfortable to anyone on board.

Oh well, the Hissa are a tough group and there is already another shuttle entering the upper atmosphere to watch. She sighs with contentment and wiggles around until she's nestled among the vines that cover the top of the slightly domed roof, staring dreamily into the night sky.

I'll make my way home before dawn, she promises herself. *No one will ever know I was gone. But for now, it's just me, the stars, and the machines.*

CHAPTER

2

Selon grunts when the shuttle finally lands, thankful to be on the ground. That was one of the worst flights he's ever had to endure, and he's eager to disembark and not get back on a shuttle for a good long time.

Besides, he wants to investigate what he saw while he was looking out the shuttle window, wondering if the pilot was going to be able to land without crashing into the control tower. He wasn't sure, but it looked like someone was lying on the roof of the tower. Common sense dictates that it's improbable, but he can't dismiss what his eyes are telling him. Just before the shuttle dropped below the tower, he'd gotten a good look. As the pilot fought with a failing thruster to keep them even, Selon strained his eyes staring at the top of the tower. Not only was he sure there was a figure there, but he could also swear it was small, like an older child.

Or a small human woman.

Could this be the famous Mara he's heard so much about? It couldn't possibly be her sister, Lara, the one so afraid of men she suffered panic attacks at their approach. Would someone so fearful be willing to roam the night alone and climb to the top of a dangerous tower with no safety gear and no protection?

Selon finds himself both intrigued and concerned.

"Good luck with the human female Lara," the pilot calls out as Selon unlocks himself from the seat and stands. He looks at the male in surprise. These are the first words the pilot has spoken since they took off back on Brimming.

"How do you know I'm here to talk to Lara?"

"Everyone knows," the pilot says with a grin. "Everyone is so interested in that female that there is a daily report on her issued planet-wide. When the Council decided to bring you back from your assignment on Brimming, they announced it. I think they are trying to remind us to be patient. This female is . . ." The pilot pauses trying to find the words. "Wounded in her mind," he finishes finally.

Selon nods. "Have you met her?"

The pilot shakes his head sadly. "Almost no one has met her. I have a cousin who works at the power plant, and he saw her there, but when he tried to approach, she screamed and almost hurt herself trying to get away. My cousin is small, like Mara's husband Tiran, and very gentle. And yet, she was still afraid."

"Fear like that can be hard to overcome," Selon explains as he opens the hatch to the shuttle. "I'll try to help, but sometimes minds never really heal."

"Just do your best," the pilot says softly. "We need her to be willing to pick a male. We all need to know there is a chance, even slight, that one of us could be the one for her."

Unwilling to give the pilot any false hope, Selon just grunts and steps off the shuttle. He looks around but only sees a few men filing into the main building. No one is looking his way. He sprints to the tower and makes his way through the foliage to the far side, where the entire stone structure is covered in thick growth. Frowning, he looks up, wondering how the female made it up there.

She's enhanced, he reminds himself. All the Decanted women are enhanced. He read all the information the Council sent him, both on the three women, Lara, Mara, and Deena as well as on the Decanting process in general. Some of the children are created to be weak and helpless as adults, but because the sisters were never supposed to grow past their child bodies, the scientists hadn't bothered limiting their genes for strength and speed. Either sister could likely make it up the vines to the top of the tower.

Tapping his shoes so they'd release his feet, he slides out of them and along with his bag, leaves them at the base of the tower. Even with his bare clawed toes to help him climb, by the time he gets to the halfway point, he's forced to stop and rest.

He, like all males, trains with the military at the citadel when he's planet-side. But not only is this not the kind of exercise he's used to, but he's been living on Brimming for quite a while. Miners are all about feats of strength, not endurance. Living and working out with the miners gave him bulk, but now he can see he'll need to rebuild his lung capacity.

He might be able to lift many times his body weight but climbing seems to be extraordinarily hard. Well, if anything, his time with the miners taught him to persevere. Miners deal with uncompromising rock all day every day. They're the very definition of stubborn. He might need to take breaks, but he's determined to make it to the top of the tower. At least the climb is giving him time to plan the meeting if it's Lara at the top instead of Mara.

And if he gets to the top and finds no one there, he'll enjoy the view, take a nap, and then find his way down.

When he finally crests the edge and eases his upper body over the rim of the tower, he sees someone relaxing among the vines. He watches the person as he moves, waiting for the small figure to notice him.

Just as he swings a leg up, she gives a startled gasp and jumps up, moving as far away from him as she can and crouching down to make herself a smaller target. Her fear tells him his instincts are correct. It's Lara on the tower.

Instead of reacting to her fear, he pretends he's struggling to get over the top. His muscles are fatigued a bit, but he exaggerates his movements, making them look uncoordinated and arduous. It's a calculated risk, and he's forced to fight his instinct because she's crouched very near the edge of the tower. He wants to snatch her up and hold her safe. But doing that would destroy any chance he has of earning her trust.

Once his whole body is on the roof, he looks up and makes eye contact with her, feigning surprise. "What are you doing here? I thought I was the only one who came up here."

She regards him with fear and suspicion. "I like it up here." The words are spoken so softly that if the wind wasn't at her back carrying her voice toward him, he might not have been able to make out what she said.

He nods solemnly. "I do too. It's fun to climb up here, although not as good as climbing up Menno Mountain. But this is much closer to where I live, so I make do." Her body is still tense, but she's not trying to move so he keeps talking. "If you like it up here, you should see Menno. It's breathtaking. No shuttles, but you can see the stars well."

"I like stars," she tells him.

He cocks his head. "I'm Selon."

She hesitates and inches back slightly. Selon clenches his fists at his side to keep from reaching out for her. She's so close to the edge that one false move and she could fall right off. He keeps talking, trying to pretend he doesn't notice her fear.

"Are you Deena, Mara, or Lara?" he asks with a forced chuckle. "You have to be one of the three, because those are the only women on all of Hissa."

His attempt at humor fails when she makes another agitated move back. Hiding his frustration, he changes tactics. "I guess it doesn't matter as long as you let me use the tower too. I'd hate to leave considering I just got back. The Council ordered everyone to stay away from you guys, so if you say so, I'll leave."

He makes his face appear sad but resigned as he reaches a leg out to feel over the edge. Lara makes a sound of distress, and he looks up. "If you go over there you can stay," she tells him and points to a section of the roof. It would make him move away from the vine-covered side of the tower so she could escape if she feels threatened.

Selon nods his head and smiles with his lips closed. Humans don't have the large biting teeth that Hissa have. They might normally show teeth in a smile, but he wants to be non-threatening, so no flashing his larger teeth. He's also careful to keep his voice calm, quiet, and even.

"Thanks, small female, for letting me enjoy the tower." He moves slowly as if unsure of his footing and even throws in a few slips hoping Lara will feel more secure if he seems ungainly and clumsy.

Once he's in the area she indicated, he settles down with a true and heartfelt sigh and stares up at the sky. He's not looking forward to the climb down!

She moves a little when he sighs, but then goes still. Even though he isn't looking directly at her, all his senses are attuned to her, and he can tell when she finally relaxes enough to move away from the edge and sits down.

Unfortunately, she sits but doesn't lie back down, a clear indicator of her wariness. However, he'll take the fact that she isn't running away from him as a significant victory. He concentrates on listening to her breathing and notes when it returns to a slower rhythmic pattern instead of the startled panting from earlier. He can hear her shift occasionally and wonders if he should have a few mats installed on the tower roof. It wouldn't be the oddest place he's ever conducted therapeutic talks, but it definitely qualifies as the highest.

"I'm Lara."

He's so content with the silence that it startles him when she speaks, and he almost sits up. He manages to keep his body still and replies casually. "Hello, Lara. Did you just see that last shuttle come in? I think the pilot was drunk."

He's rewarded with a stifled giggle. "Not drunk."

"How can you be so sure?"

"It was overloaded," she informs him, voice soft but confident. "These guys do that a lot. Overload the cargo shuttles."

"I didn't know that," he tells her honestly. He wants to look at her but keeps his eyes focused on the sky and yet another ship coming in. "You know, they're full of minerals from the moons."

No response. She's gone silent. He doesn't say anything more, just lets the silence stretch. She needs to decide the pace of the conversation, any pushing from him will only make her draw back both physically and mentally. He needs to tread carefully, mindful of her fear.

"Do you come here often?"

Selon isn't sure how to answer. He doesn't want to lie. Instead, he verbally steps sideways. "I've been on the moon. I just got back tonight."

There's a long silence until she finally asks, "Which one?"

"The bigger one, Brimming, the one farther away. You can't see it now. It'll probably rise in a few hours." Silence descends again, and he listens to her breathing.

"I like ships," she volunteers. The incoming cargo shuttle sways a little and dips dangerously. Selon is starting to wonder if someone should speak to the Council about load size. This is dangerous.

He pauses before he speaks, weighing his words carefully. "You like to watch ships?"

"Sure," she says easily. "And to work on them."

Selon doesn't need to fake the surprise in his voice. "You can work on them?"

"I can fix anything." There's no pride in her voice, just fact. "I'm really good."

That wasn't included in the file the Council sent him. They probably saw her past profession as irrelevant. Idiots.

Now's he's genuinely curious. "What would you do about these cargo shuttles?"

It takes her so long to answer that he wonders if she's going to. Then she finally speaks. The way she talks tells him she hesitated because she was deciding on whether to give him an honest answer or not.

"They either need to load a third less weight or add a secondary booster system. They probably handle easily on the moons, but down here it's a whole different thing. I bet a lot of ships burn out prematurely under the strain. Crashes have to be common because the pilots can't know when a ship is going to lose engines. You know, because of being so overworked. I wonder why the pilots don't complain."

That's a question Selon can answer. "They don't want to be seen as weak. They are probably afraid complaining will make them appear unskilled or cowardly."

"That's dumb," she responds without any pause. "You should tell someone. You're not a pilot, and now you know how to fix the problem. You don't have to worry about being seen as those things." The fact that she's not weighing her words tells him she's rapidly starting to relax in his presence.

"I'll try, but I'm not a pilot or an engineer. They're unlikely to listen to me," he tells her and then decides to push a little. "Would you be willing to help put boosters on one? If I ask, they might be willing to test a single cargo shuttle to see if it's a viable option."

He can almost hear her body get tense at his words. He's pushed too hard and now needs to backpedal. "No, that's a bad idea. Forget I asked. You're probably too busy."

That must have struck a chord with her because she shifts restlessly as she talks. "I guess I could do one to show how it works. As long as no one bothers me. I'd need space. No helper and lots of space."

That demand makes Selon see the flaw in his plan. "But you couldn't lift a booster by yourself. You'd need help." He expects her to retract her offer or show anxiety and dismay. She does none of those things. Instead, she sounds an indelicate snort.

That derisive sound fills his heart with joy. This little human might be fighting a battle against her panic, but she's not so far gone that she can't be disdainful.

"They aren't that heavy," she says, her voice full of mild scorn. "And it's not like I'm going to try to just lift them myself. None of your lot would be able to lift an entire engine either, I'm sure. No one can. Well, maybe several of you working together, but that's just silly when you can use an ambulatory stand." She makes a soft humming sound, then shares a memory with him. "That's what I did when we had to replace engine three on Ally. Deena rented an ambulatory stand for me along with an enclosed bay. It wasn't easy because the stand almost collapsed sideways. I spent a long time fixing the stand before I could even get to the engine. But I'm sure you have better equipment here."

"Have you been given a tour of the port yet?" he asks.

"Yes, but they wouldn't take me in any of the repair areas. They said it was too dangerous." Her tone is sullen and frustrated. He doesn't blame the men who refused. She probably asked in a quiet fearful voice and acting with an overabundance of caution, they denied her access.

None could know that her request came from a place of deep curiosity and not just a passing interest.

"What's your favorite type of cargo shuttle?" he asks, expecting her to wax poetic about a specific ship.

"I like just about anything with a Cavinoria class two engine," she says.

"I'm sorry, what?" he asks, thoroughly lost. That makes her giggle.

"Cavinoria makes great engines. Sturdy, reliable, and usually pretty easy to work on. Their class two isn't as popular because it's on the smaller size, but its power to cubic-size ratio is phenomenal!"

"Power to cubic-size? Are you speaking Space Standard? Because nothing you just said made any sense." His humorous reaction makes her laugh. For him, her soft laughter is like winning a prize.

She's so relaxed in his presence she can laugh.

"You know how mass, weight, and heaviness aren't issues in space because of the whole no-gravity, no-friction thing. That means engines built to use in spaceships aren't judged by their power to weight ratio. Instead, we judge them by how much power they can put out in relation to how much space they take up on a ship. The more space an engine takes up, the less cargo or fewer people you can fit. Anyway . . ."

Listening with half an ear, he lets her explain the

interactives of ships, engines, and why Cavinorias are the best engines on the market. While she talks, he plans.

The topic of engines and ships allows her to speak so effortlessly. She probably doesn't realize it, but her voice has gotten stronger and more assured as she talks about the Cavinoria engines. No hesitation between sentences. No weighing words. No indications of stress or anxiety.

This gives him valuable insight into helping her. She's obviously used to being busy and the enforced inactivity on Hissa is probably starting to get to her. But driven by her need to blend in and her fear of men, it's unlikely anyone knows she feels restless. Her restlessness might be his key to getting her to talk to him.

When she starts talking fondly of all the issues with her old ship the Ally, he thinks about the missive he'll write to the Council requesting space and materials for Lara. Then he hears her give a small laugh and that pulls him completely out of his thoughts.

"Deena was so pissed that it failed even before we undocked. We didn't have to pay for the part, and she even managed to get a few credits out of the deal. Deena's good at that, getting people to do things." He missed the part of the story where she explained what she was fixing, but that's inconsequential. The important thing is that she's sharing freely, relaxed and unconcerned.

"I've heard about Deena," Selon murmurs. "From the sound of it, she's not one to trifle with."

He hears her move a little and tenses, thinking he's scared her somehow, but when he looks over, she's peering at him curiously. "What have you heard? About Deena, I mean."

He shrugs and looks away. "I heard she's been having a great time with Hissa males. None of them are complaining, but I guess she's a little wild."

Lara barks out a laugh, and then clamps both hands over her mouth as if worried there might be repercussions from the sound. The movement and wild, watchful eyes make Selon's heart hurt. He hurries to try and bring back the humor of moments before. "I've also heard she likes to fly."

Lara lowers her hands and nods enthusiastically, eager to talk about her friend. "She loves to fly. She's the best pilot you'll ever meet."

Selon smiles at her earnest words. "It makes sense you two would be friends: one likes to fly and the other likes to fix. Perfect match."

Lara nods again but doesn't say anything. Selon watches

the smaller moon make its way across the sky and thinks about
how late it is. He needs to be the first to leave or Lara won't feel
safe enough to climb down from her perch. Besides, he's got a lot
of people to wake up and plans to set in motion.

He sits up, ignoring her startled reaction, and stretches his
arms out with an exaggerated yawn.

"It's been very pleasant," he tells her and makes sure not to
look directly at her as he moves to the side of the tower. It's not
until he's gotten both legs over the edge of the tower that he meets
her gaze. "I'm tired, and I need to go to bed. Please be careful,
Lara. Enjoy the rest of your night."

She makes a small sound. He pretends she just answered
him back as he starts the long trek down. Out of the corner of his
eye, he watches her peek out over the edge of the tower, watching
him descend. That's why, when he gets to the bottom, he
deliberately takes his time putting on his shoes and grabbing his
bag. He needs to show her that he's unconcerned with her being on
the tower, that he's not going to rush off to tell people. The more
he acts like this is normal, the more she'll trust him. To that end, he
strides off toward the closest tram until he knows he's out of sight.

Dropping his bag, he runs around the large building until
he gets to the thick patch of vegetation that covers one side of the
tower. He settles himself down in the shadows and waits. It's a
long time before Lara makes her way down, and he can't help but
admire her grace. He didn't get a good look at her when they were
talking, but now he can take his time and study her.

Long limbs make easy work of the tower as she flows
down like a dancer descending a stage. When she lands at the
bottom, she's standing in a pool of light, and Selon almost gasps at
his first good look at her.

He's transfixed by her beauty. Large golden eyes set in a
delicate face look nothing like the haunted fearful ones in the
pictures he was sent. Her shoulder-length black hair shines in the
light and Selon just knows it would be soft to the touch. Suddenly,
he wants to step out of the shadows and touch her so badly his
hands start shaking.

Desperate for control, he punches his fist into the dirt
around him, making a soft thud.

Lara swings around, startled, her wide eyes frantically
searching the shadows. Selon keeps himself perfectly still, and
finally she blows out the breath she's been holding. She doesn't see
him and has dismissed the sound.

Turning, she moves off, her pace quick but not panicked.

Selon waits for a few beats, then eases out of the vegetation to follow her. She runs smoothly, covering ground with ease. He's forced to sprint from hiding spot to hiding spot to follow her without being seen. At one point, he thinks he might have lost her but then turns a corner to find her ducking into a covered doorway. He just barely catches himself and manages to stop and move back so she can't see him from where she hides.

He follows her line of sight and sees two males pulling a large mechanism from a slot in the side of a building. They're maintenance doing their evening job. He waits, interested to see what Lara will do.

She watches the men work, and it takes a moment for him to realize she's learning their movements. When both their backs are turned to move the machine, Lara darts away and is long gone before either man might turn and catch sight of her. She has a gift for hiding, and now he understands how no one's caught on to her late-night jaunts.

He wants to run after her, but because of the maintenance crew, she'll be more cautious now, looking behind her more often. If he follows right away, she'll see him. Even though he knows there's no real danger for her here on Hissa, his instinct to protect her is strong, and it's a fight to remain still and potentially lose her in the night.

This experience is also a revelation for him. With all her fear, running around, and hiding, she's no doubt been driving the protective instincts of all the Hissa men around her crazy. This is an excellent example of a negative feedback loop. Hissa men want to protect her, so they get close. She gets scared and tries to run, so they become even more protective and get even closer.

When she's out of sight, he sprints after her and just catches her scent. He follows that until he's got her in visual range again. She's back to her loping pace, covering ground but not pushing herself too hard. He wonders at the adrenaline issue both sisters share and hopes it wasn't triggered when she saw the men.

All too soon, she turns away from the path and to a family dwelling. He's not surprised when she avoids the front door where two imposing Hissa guards stand vigilant. Ducking behind a convenient coppice of Bantino trees, he watches as she circles around to the side of the house. It's well-known that Decanted women are stronger than regular human women, so Selon shouldn't be surprised when she manages to leap twelve feet in the air. Still, he finds himself taking in a sharp breath as he watches her demonstrate both agility and strength by catching the windowsill with only the tips of her fingers. Without too much apparent effort, she pulls herself up and slides silently through the open window, disappearing into the dark house.

Giving himself a moment, he leans against a tree trunk and slides to the ground with a little sigh of relief. It's a testament to his training that he was able to remain still and silent as she displayed her physical prowess. He's sure most Hissa men would've rushed to snatch her out of the air and demand she not do such dangerous things.

Most Hissa men wouldn't have let her stay on the tower.

By the moon, no Hissa man would let her wander out in the night, alone.

From the accounts he's read, Mara might not like being inactive, but she isn't afraid to voice her opinion or frustrations with her mate Tiran or the Council. That's why Mara gets access to her ship Witch and gets to go out hiking and camping in the jungle alone with Tiran. But he's sure Lara never complains. She might be dying of fear, anxiety, and frustration, but all anyone sees is the helpless female that cowers away from them.

But she's not helpless, she's just wounded. And wounds can heal. If she has the courage to sneak out of her house at night on a planet full of big males, just so she can watch ships come and go, then she's not as broken as the Council thinks she is.

He hears a hiss as her bedroom window shuts and seals. That tells Selon she's probably done wandering for the night.

"Sleep well, little climber," he murmurs to the dark window. "We have a lot of hard work ahead of us."

CHAPTER

3

Lara slowly eats her bowl of fruit as Mara and Tiran argue. She watches them out of the corner of her eye, unwilling to risk direct eye contact with Tiran. On the rare occasion he talks directly to her, he's polite and keeps his voice soft, but for some reason, it always seems like he's ordering her around. She doesn't like that. She doesn't like to be told what to do.

Deena never ordered her around. With Deena it was a partnership. They talked. They figured out what needed to happen to survive. Deena never dismissed her, even when it was hard for her to find the words. Even when her throat wanted to close, and it was almost impossible to get the words out. Deena always waited.

But Tiran doesn't like to wait, and he makes impatient sounds when she doesn't talk. And his face scrunches up with frustration; then the blue scale pattern on his head starts to darken toward brown. Those are all bad signs. Those are all indicators of a Hissa about to lose his temper.

And right now, he's displaying those signs. At least they aren't focused on her. No, they're focused on Mara, her much stronger and braver twin sister. At least Mara can give as good as she gets. Which she demonstrates by slapping both her hands flat on Tiran's chest and shoving. Not surprisingly, Tiran doesn't even move, which only seems to annoy Mara more.

"I need something to do!" Mara states for the fifth time in as many minutes, pushing at him again, this time with a little more force. "I'm not used to having nothing to do. I'm going crazy here."

It's very clear the moment Tiran decides to take a different tact in this argument. His face relaxes, the scale pattern on his head goes from brown to blue and toward purple, and he grins, showing off his long canines.

"I can give you plenty to do," Tiran says and reaches for her. Mara evades him easily, then puts the table Lara's sitting at between her and Tiran. He doesn't chase her, instead just watches, smile still in place.

Mara puts her hands on her hips, and Lara can see her sister is fighting not to smile. "Don't get me wrong, that's fun too. But when you're off working or at meetings with the council, I'm stuck here, bored."

"What about keeping Lara company? That's important," Tiran points out, and Lara watches all humor disappear from Mara's face. That makes her want to speak up. He shouldn't be using her against Mara. That's underhanded and unnecessary.

Right, this is for her sister. She's going to talk. She's going to tell Tiran he can't use her as a source of emotional blackmail. She thinks about the words she's going to say. Repeats them half a dozen times in her head. Then, when she's sure she can get the words out, she looks up only to find both Tiran and Mara staring at her.

Now she can't even get enough words out to ask them to look away. All sound is frozen deep in her chest. Her words and thoughts are trapped. Again.

When he frowns, she quickly looks away, focusing on her half empty bowl. She wasn't even hungry when she fixed the food. She only ate because Deena bugged her about it. Now look at what's happened: she tried to please Deena and got trapped in the kitchen with an arguing Tiran and Mara.

When he makes an impatient sound, words do finally emerge from her, but they aren't the ones she wanted to say.

"I should go," she whispers. How predictable of her. She won't be voicing any demands today.

Mara puts a gentle hand on her shoulder. "This isn't about you," Mara assures her. "I love spending time with you." Lara looks up to her sister and nods, trying to control her fears and show her sister a brave face. For a moment, having Mara there gives her the courage to talk.

"I'm a burden. I shouldn't be a burden. I can work too." The statement comes out as a plea, and Tiran makes a disapproving sound. Hunching her shoulders, she abandons her food and stumbles away from the table.

Tiran blocks her exit. "I'm not angry at you, Lara. It's just the idea of you working doesn't sit well with me. You should be resting and healing, not laboring." His tone is gruff, but at least he's not shouting.

She nods quickly without looking up, using her shaggy hair to hide her face. She waits, gripping her arms around her waist, hoping he'll step aside so she can pass. There's only one door to the kitchen area, and unless she goes out the window, she's trapped.

Tiran sighs and steps aside so she can scamper out of the kitchen and down the hall to her room. The room isn't small enough to comfort her, so she goes into the closet and closes the door behind her. She took all the shelves and storage cabinets out of the closet days ago and filled it with bedding. Most nights this is where she sleeps. The closet reminds her of the small, make-shift room on Ally. It feels a little safer.

Not sure what else to do, she curls up in her bedding and listens to the sounds of muted voices below. It sounds like Deena's joined the conversation. Maybe she can tell Tiran to let Mara work.

"And she'll be in her closet for a while," Deena mutters as she enters the room. She eyes Tiran and Mara and then shakes her head. "You guys need to leave her out of your little tiffs. You're dealing with her all wrong."

Mara glowers at Deena. "And you've done such a great job of dealing with her fear?"

Deena knows Mara's angry because she feels responsible for Lara's damaged mind, so she doesn't rise to the bait. Instead, she picks up the bowl of fruit Lara left and starts munching. "I have," she states simply.

Tiran grabs Mara before she can launch herself across the

table. Deena just smirks at her. "Bad Mara," she admonishes. "It's not polite to start fights in the house."

Tiran frowns at her. "That's not helpful Deena."

Deena feels a little jolt of shame and then dismisses it. These two might have Lara's best intentions at heart, but they're going about everything all wrong. Their bumbling has just made everything worse. Deena's never been one to pull punches, so why start now? "Look, I've told you what you need to do, but you don't listen to me."

Tiran's frown deepens. "There's no job she could have where she wouldn't be surrounded by males."

"Then build her a shop and let her tinker with stuff. I'm sure small appliances break all the time. She loves fixing those things. She calls them 'candy fixes' because they're so much easier to work on than big complex ship machinery."

Mara cocks her head at that. "What does she call ship engines?"

"Headaches," Deena tells her succinctly, and Mara laughs.

"Let go, big guy," she tells Tiran, tapping one of his arms holding her back from attacking Deena. "I'm done being angry." Tiran lets her drop to the ground. Mara stands, staring at Deena, then huffs out a breath and throws herself into a seat. Tiran takes a seat next to her at the table.

"Fine," Mara plucks a piece of fruit from Deena's bowl. "Anything else?"

"She needs to feel safe," Deena starts, hoping they'll listen to her this time.

"You've said that," Tiran points out. "The Council issued rules specific to her. Men aren't knocking at our door anymore, and guards are always posted. And she has escorts wherever she goes."

Deena rolls her eyes. "That's not what I meant."

Tiran doesn't get angry or defensive. To her surprise, he nods for her to continue. "Then tell us what you mean."

Deena takes a deep breath, then lets it out, showing she's not as relaxed as she's pretending to be. She's been waiting for them to realize that their approach to Lara isn't working. Now she needs to make them understand what will work.

"She needs a hidey-hole. A place she can climb or jump into that any of us would find way too cramped, or too high and difficult to make it into. It makes her feel secure when she knows she has a place like that to retreat to."

"What about the closet in her room?" Mara asks. "She's already set up a bed in there to sleep."

Deena shakes her head. "Not good enough. It needs to be high with a small opening. She created a room on Ally just above the bridge as her spot. I'm not sure what the room housed originally, but she rerouted a bunch of stuff and did a lot of work to turn it into her bedroom. There were only two openings and both of them were small. One of the openings was a square panel she fixed with a latch and hinges in the floor of her room. She could drop into the bridge from there. She didn't mean to, but she scared me all the time, dropping down right behind the pilot chair," Deena chuckles at the memory. "She could jump back up if she needed to, latch the door, and it would look just like the rest of the ceiling paneling. That's what she needs."

Tiran sits back, thoughtful. "I can have a small room built on the roof."

Deena shrugs. "That might work. It would be better if it could be something on stilts, something hard to get into."

They all fall silent, thinking until Tiran sits up with a grin. "Tiran house!"

Deena and Mara eye him with confusion. "Yes," Deena says with deliberate slowness, as if speaking to someone without all their mental faculties. "We are in your house."

Tiran shakes his head, chuckling. "No. Sorry, sometimes I get my Space Standard and Hissa words mixed together. My name means tree. I meant tree house. When I was a child, my mother built me a small house in a tree, and I would climb up there and pretend it was a ship."

Deena leans forward with interest. "Your house is almost surrounded by big trees. That's not a bad idea. Especially if you can make it close to her bedroom window. She could jump from the window into the treehouse and then close the treehouse door. That kind of restricted access will make her feel pretty secure."

Tiran frowns and shakes his head. "Absolutely no jumping. She could miss, fall, and hurt herself."

Deena sits back and makes a little frustrated sound. That just felt like she took two steps forward and then a step back.

"Are they all like this?" she asks Mara and is rewarded when the other woman nods in the affirmative and shoots Tiran an exasperated look.

"It's like we are made of glass, ready to shatter at any moment," Mara confirms.

Denna looks back at Tiran and shrugs. "Fine, then put a small gangplank across from the roof to the tree house. It needs to be just strong enough for her weight though. She won't feel safe if just anyone can cross it."

Comprehension shows on Tiran's face as he nods. "I think I understand now. This would be her little fortress, not just a place to hide."

"Right!" For the first time in days, Deena feels a real smile form on her face. "From the little she's told me; she spent a lot of time in a situation where she was constantly looking for a place she could hide and feel safe. It's important to her that she's got something like that. I think that's why there are so many nightmares right now."

Mara leans forward, her face equal parts sadness and interest. "What do you know about her past?"

Deena sighs and shrugs. She knew they would ask and although she doesn't feel right telling Lara's story without her permission, she also knows her brilliant mechanic is unlikely to tell them any time soon.

"I only know bits and pieces," Deena admits. "Stuff she said coming out of nightmares or when she got a little drunk once. When your ship got attacked and you two launched in separate life pods, you might have ended up being picked up by the Fielden, but Lara's pod was grabbed by the raiders. She spent a year on that ship, property of the captain."

Tiran and Mara share expressions of abject horror. "Poor Lara," Mara whispers, tears in her eyes. Tiran reaches out to hug her, drawing her into his lap. Deena ignores their easy affection and orders herself not to be jealous. She had a husband once, and it was horrible. She'll never be trapped like that again.

"She once told me she was lucky the captain didn't share her, unlike all the other captives they picked up during the time she was with them. I guess none of them lasted long because the crew was so rough on them," Deena can't help but give a little shudder. Everyone at the table has heard stories of how raiders treat captives, both men and women. For most of them, death was probably a welcome relief.

"I know she would disappear into the engine rooms a lot. She was so much smaller than most of the crew they wouldn't be able to get to her. The captain could call her back, though, because his voice was linked to her obedience collar."

Mara scowls. "I hate those damn collars."

"I can imagine," Deena says with a grimace, thankful she's never been forced to wear one.

"She told me she always liked to take stuff apart and put it back together, so while she was hiding in the engine, she'd start tinkering. Soon she was assigned there full time unless the captain wanted her in his quarters. They even gave her access to the ship's systems and manuals. It made her life a little better I think."

"She's always been smart," Mara murmurs and leans her head against Tiran's chest. "I was the one who couldn't be still. She could sit and read for hours. I always thought it was boring."

Deena sits back, the bowl empty. "That's all I know. She's the finest mechanic I've ever worked with. Let her fix things. It'll make her happy."

Tiran's about to open his mouth when he hears the front door alarm sound. "I think that must be Selon. He's an exceptionally skilled Mind Mender. Probably our best. The Council called him back from the second moon especially for her."

He stands up, gives Mara one last hug, and reluctantly sets her back on her feet. They all follow him to the front entrance. Deena can see Lara peering out from a crack in her bedroom door. She almost grins. *I'm fighting for you,* she thinks. *Just don't stop fighting for yourself.*

CHAPTER

4

Selon waits nervously for someone to open the door. He knows it's unlikely to be Lara but worries anyway. When the large round door swings open to reveal Tiran and two human females, he almost sighs with relief. Lara isn't among the people at the door.

Mara stands next to Tiran, long black hair flowing down her back, unlike Lara's shorter, spikier, shoulder-length haircut. Even without the difference in hair lengths, it would still be easy to tell the sisters apart despite their identical features. Mara stands proud, tall, and undaunted next to her Hissa mate. Her shoulders are back. Her eyes are up and challenging. Her confidence is in stark contrast to Lara's timid fearful nature.

Next to Mara stands Deena, the pilot. Despite being from the same line of Decanted Children, she looks nothing like the two sisters. She's smaller, with a much rounder body and darker skin than the pale twins. Her large brown eyes are hard and intractable, a notable contrast to the contours of her soft body.

"Selon?" Tiran asks as all three step back to allow him inside. He moves forward quickly and grabs Tiran's arm before he can move too much further into the house. He knows what he's about to do might not be entirely ethical, but hopes the ends justify the means.

All three freeze when he grabs Tiran's arm, and he can see Mara's hands clench into fists, ready to defend her mate. *Ah,* he thinks, *so the rumors of her being a fighter are true.*

"No time to explain," he tells them quickly in a whisper. "Just go along with me, please."

All three are giving him confused looks and he can tell they're all about to start asking questions. He knows Lara must be somewhere behind them in the shadows, watching and waiting. He straightens and speaks a little louder than necessary.

"The Council sent me. They'd like to request Lara install a booster assembly on one of the cargo shuttles to see if it can compensate for the heavy loads coming from the mining colonies on the moons. I told them the loads needed to be lighter, but they're unwilling to do that. After I pointed out that we're putting our pilots in undue danger, they agreed to try a booster assembly on one cargo shuttle as proof of concept. After reading Deena's report on Lara's skill set, I suggested Lara be the one to install it. We don't have any others who can take the time for such a task at the moment."

Not everything he's saying is a complete lie, but a lot of it is stretching the truth so thin that it would be transparent if it was a material object. But the risk he's taking is rewarded when they hear a little gasp of delight from the back of the house.

He grins as the three of them regard him. Tiran looks mildly angry; Deena is beaming at him; and Mara looks confused.

Mara leans forward and whispers, "How did you know?"

"I'll explain later," he promises, hoping Tiran will stop glaring.

"I don't think this is a good idea," Tiran begins to say in a normal voice, but Selon cuts him off, keeping his voice pleasant but firm.

"It isn't your choice to make. The contract is being offered to Lara Stray, sister of Mara Lost. Only she can accept or decline the contract."

After Lara was safely ensconced in her room last night, he woke several members of the Council and outlined a plan to help in her healing. There was pushback at first, but it's amazing how much cooperation you can get when you display an abundance of confidence.

Just as the sun was ready to rise, he finished convincing enough of the Council members to finally get permission for his less than normal treatment plan. Then he spent the first half of the day arranging for the space, tools, parts, and a shuttle for her to work on. Now, with the day halfway behind them, he's eager to give her this opportunity he knows she desperately wants.

"Have we met?" Deena asks him. "Because you're pushy and you just annoyed Tiran. On top of that, you're somehow getting Lara access to muck about with engines. That means you just might be my new favorite Hissa."

"We have not met yet," he tells her with the grin he's been practicing in the mirror. It allows his lips to move up but doesn't show any teeth. He feels it's important that he appear as non-threatening as possible. That's why he also donned gloves to hide his claws. He's also wearing loose clothing in soft shades of blue, sandals instead of boots, and is carrying several colorful cloth bags in his hands. He hopes the whole effect will not only make his appearance less aggressive, but with his hands full he might even look harmless.

"Can you get me in the pilot seat again?" Deena asks.

"I have no control over that," he says honestly. Deena's demands to be allowed to pilot are well known, and the Council keeps going back and forth about whether it should be allowed or not. However, Deena is bold enough to make her wishes known, loudly and repeatedly. She doesn't need him to advocate for her like Lara does. "You'll need to keep negotiating with the Council, I'm afraid. I'm only here to ask Lara if she'd be willing to work for us at the port."

As they've been talking, Lara's been gathering her courage. Selon can just see a figure stepping out of a room and taking several hesitant steps down the hall toward them. *That's it,* he thinks. *I have something you want. Be brave enough to accept it. That's all you need to do.*

Tiran is saying something to him, but his entire focus is on Lara, trying to see all of her without looking directly at her. He waits, pretending to listen to Tiran refusing on behalf of Lara, silently encouraging the woman still hidden in the hall to speak up.

"Please," she says so softly Selon is sure he's the only one who heard her. But Deena swings around at the plea and acts quickly.

"Hi, honey," she calls out, motioning her forward eagerly. "Looks like they need your help. Would you mind working on a cargo shuttle? I'm dying to fly, and if you agree to help out, I bet I can get them to let me do the test flight. Please do this for me?"

Selon smothers a smile, Deena's good. She just manipulated the whole situation. Now, by working on the shuttle, Lara will feel like she's being good to her friend as well as getting to do the kind of work she loves.

Just like last night, Lara's hair hangs over her face, making it hard to read her expression as she takes another small, slow step forward. "I can do that, but I don't want helpers." Selon could just shout with happiness. Not only is Lara accepting the job, but she's already making requests.

"There's no reason you should be called on to do this at all," Tiran objects. Selon knows the words stem from fear for Lara's safety, but he feels the urge to punch the male for making her hunch her shoulders and take a step back. Thankfully, Mara intercedes.

"Sure, there is," Mara says, catching on quickly. Elbowing her mate hard enough to make him wince, she keeps her voice light and cheerful. "I bet she's the best mechanic on Hissa." Mara shoots a warning look at Tiran, then turns to address her sister. "You don't need to worry about us. Tiran would be delighted if you wanted to work on the shuttle." Another hard jab makes Tiran huff out a breath.

"Delighted," Tiran echoes with a smile at Mara, showing more teeth than strictly necessary.

Lara takes another tentative step forward. "You'll go with me?" Her eyes are focused on him, her head tilted slightly as she asks.

All three turn to stare at Selon, and he struggles to keep his face neutral. Tiran and Mara look shocked, while Deena gives him a curious look. "I could keep you company if that's what you want."

"As long as you give me space," she says softly with a little nod, as if she's saying the same thing to herself as well as him. "I can do this as long as you're there, but don't get too close. No guards. No helpers." He sees a hint of a smile through the hair that obscures most of her features.

Because of their interactions at the tower and now his offer for something she wants, they've created trust between them. She could have requested Deena, but having the pilot bored and restless with her all day in a hangar probably isn't the most pleasant thought. Used to being busy, the pilot wouldn't have the patience to sit and watch Lara work. And from what he's read, when this woman gets bored, she starts trouble. A good reason to leave her behind.

And of course, she wouldn't want Mara to come because then there's a good chance Tiran would be there too. But she can't be alone. There's no way Tiran, Mara, or the Council would allow that, and she knows it. That makes him the best alternative out of very few options.

He tries very hard not to read too much into her choice. He's safe. He's already proven he can be trusted to keep his distance. To remain silent. To respect her fears.

All of that will help him unravel the damage done to her so many years ago. If he's lucky, he can help her heal. Set her mind on a path where panic isn't the most common reaction to unexpected stimuli.

Suddenly she frowns. "I don't have any tools. They were all lost when Ally exploded."

"I'm sure they have tools at the port," Deena volunteers quickly, obviously eager to see her friend engaged in an activity she enjoys so much. "And if they don't have what you need, I'm sure they can get it. Besides, you're used to making do with whatever is on hand anyway."

Lara grins at Deena. "True, I worked for a cheapskate captain for years." Her voice is barely above a whisper, but the love and comradery there is hard to miss.

Deena laughs at the old joke and points out the door. "Get going. That booster won't install itself!"

Selon steps back through the doorway and makes sure to give Lara plenty of room to step out. There's a tense moment when Tiran doesn't move to allow Lara to pass, but with a move too fast to follow, Mara does something, making Tiran wince and step aside. He allows Lara to pass without saying anything more.

Stepping forward, Mara gives her a quick hug. "I'll be down a little later to check on you. And bring you food. You didn't eat any breakfast, and you left your lunch half eaten."

Lara awkwardly returns the hug while nodding her head.

"Should I call Penon or Woken?" Tiran asks softly, and Selon sees Lara freeze.

"No, it's unnecessary," Selon assures him quickly. "I brought a private transport, and we'll ride it into the repair bay. No one will see her, and that bay is now strictly off-limits to everyone but the five of us."

Lara starts moving again and stops just in front of Selon. "I'm ready," she says simply in a quiet voice, her head slightly bowed, her hair covering her features.

For Lara that's downright bold.

Tiran glares: Mara looks happy but concerned; and Deena smirks. Deena's obvious delight forces Selon to smother a grin of his own. He extends his arm toward the waiting transport. "This way please." Then he turns and starts walking, confident she'll follow him.

He gets in first and waits patiently when she hesitates at the door. He knows she doesn't want to be trapped in a small space with him. The question is, will her desire to work on the shuttle win over her trepidation?

"I'm not sure we got the correct assembly," he tells her casually, pulling a small data pad out of one of the bags he's carrying. Tapping the screen until the schematics for the booster are displayed. "One of the pilots said he wanted this one, but now I'm worried it might not do the job."

One of her hands twitches a little, and she climbs in after him, her attention focused on the data pad. He holds it out to her and feels their fingers brush as she takes it. She gives a little startled sound, then tucks herself into the corner of the transport and focuses on the data pad.

Selon ignores the flash of heat that moved through him at her touch. He orders the transport to the port and then turns to face the window, pretending to be absorbed in his thoughts while Lara grips the data pad so tightly her fingers turn white. The small interior of the transport is no place to push Lara.

It's not long before the transport is neatly parking in a large repair bay, the door automatically opening with a chime. Selon waits patiently for Lara to move out of the transport before he does and forces himself to keep a sedate pace as she scrambles across the bay to the waiting cargo shuttle. The transport closes its door, starts back up, and leaves the same way it came. Neither one of them pay any attention.

"Oh, it's just lovely," she sighs with a soft voice, running her hand down the side of the shuttle. Then she notices a black stain near an engine and gives a small sound of distress.

"This engine needs an overhaul. It's been pushed too hard." Then she starts grumbling about stupid pilots as she continues her inspection.

Selon makes sure to stay out of her way, but close enough to hear all her words as she fusses at the state of the engine and shuttle. He doesn't understand half of what she's saying but is entertained by the way she talks to the shuttle. She's acting as if it's a living, breathing thing. She's talking to it like it's a beloved pet.

"Don't worry. I'm going to fix you right up. Good as new. I bet your intake manifold is just full of muck. I'll get it nice and clean. And all your filters. I bet they never did a tolerance test for your steering gimbal either. Stupid, stupid, stupid."

Once she's satisfied with her initial inspection, she turns to Selon and takes a bold step toward him. He isn't expecting her to be this relaxed this quickly and makes sure to remain still as she draws close.

"I need things," she states. She is looking at him through her hair, but at least she is looking directly at him. She starts to list the things she needs, and Selon takes half a step back and holds up his hands in mock surrender.

"Could you please record it on the data pad? I don't even know what most of the things you just named are!"

To his astonishment, she gives a soft giggle and looks down at the data pad still in her hands. "Sorry," she says. "I used to do that to Deena all the time too. I should know better."

Going back to mumbling, she starts tapping on the data pad with her small fingers. When she's finished, she steps close enough to hold the pad out to him. Both of them ignore the fact that her hand is shaking as he takes the pad from her.

"I might need more things than this," she warns him, taking a large step back the moment he closes his fingers around the device.

"That shouldn't be a problem," he assures her. She might have stepped back, but she's looking him in the eye. Her shoulders are only a little slumped, and her hands are in her pockets instead of wrapped around her waist. Those are all good signs, but the most important thing is that she's smiling.

CHAPTER

¨ ¨
5

Lara hasn't felt this good in weeks. The bay is full of tools, and the cargo shuttle in front of her needs a great deal of maintenance before she'll even consider retrofitting the booster onto it. Which is good because the booster won't even get there for another few days.

With a grin of pure delight, she starts pulling the access panels off the engine and assessing the abused shuttle. Selon keeps a respectable distance, watching with interest as she tugs off access panels and carefully sets them down in an orderly fashion.

She likes Selon. He's calm.

Every other Hissa she's met so far, aside from Tiran, are frantic around her. Of course, while Tiran might not be frantic, he isn't pleasant either. He's always glowering at her and ordering her away from things.

All the rest of the Hissa men seem to want her attention. The men approach her with frenzied enthusiasm. Then they touch her. They can't seem to help but touch her. When she and Deena first arrived, they even grabbed her because they were so desperate to gain her attention. The first few days on Hissa were a nightmare.

But things calmed as the Council created protocol about meeting her or being around her. That helped, but it didn't fix everything. Males are still desperate to see her. Talk to her. Touch her. Beg her to just spend one evening with them.

Even her guards, who are always nice and respectful, look at her with longing and hope. Whenever they are alone with her, they try and entice her to visit their homes or some other attraction on Hissa. It's not uncommon for the guards assigned to her to get into verbal sparring matches over why she should pick one or the other.

Those memories make her cringe. Once the verbal turned into the physical and the guards had to be separated. She was told they were reassigned off-planet, but their violent fighting made her distrustful of any of the guards.

She's not allowed to leave the house without them. But going anywhere with them is anxiety-inducing at best because she's just waiting for them to either make advances toward her or fight with each other. That's why she hasn't been out of the house in days. At least not with an escort. If anyone found out about her nighttime escapades, she's sure not only would she be reprimanded, but they'd also take steps to make sure she couldn't do it anymore.

They're all just trying to make her safe. Make her comfortable. But they're making her feel trapped.

These thoughts make her sigh as she gently lays a panel on the ground.

"Are those too heavy?"

Lara looks up, startled. She momentarily forgot Selon was there. He's such a quiet, easy presence that she doesn't feel the need to be constantly on guard around him. He's not going to frown and tell her no. He's not going to get into a fight with another male. He's not going to demand she accept gifts she doesn't want. No, he's going to mind his own business when he meets a lone female late at night on a vine-covered tower. He's going to listen attentively when she talks and asks questions but not give advice. And he's going to leave and let her find her way home when she's ready.

Selon might be the perfect Hissa.

She smiles to reassure him. "No, they're light." Then she thinks of something else and frowns a little, "Are you bored? I know someone has to be with me, but I'd rather you stay than Woken, Penon, or anyone else. They're all very nice. But I'd like you to stay instead."

Anyone but Woken. That Hissa is a walking building. He makes other Hissa look short. Most Hissa are around seven to seven and a half feet tall but not Woken. Oh no, he's a mountain among hills. He towers over everyone, and she guesses he's somewhere around eight feet tall. He's almost so tall she needs to start using yards instead of feet. Woken might never have raised his voice around her, but his sheer size makes all the breath disappear from her lungs.

But really, it's not just about the size that makes her want Selon rather than anyone else. This male is special. She wants to tell him that, but she doesn't want him to think she's making an advance.

Frowning, she tries to explain. "It's just that you're easy. I mean, easy to talk to. That's why I want you to stay."

"Thank you for the compliment. I'd be happy to stay," Selon assures her with a smile of his own. Lara's caught by that smile. His body stands relaxed, his attitude serene, and Lara finds his tranquility has a stabilizing effect on her. He's even standing close enough to reach out and touch, but she doesn't feel intimated or worried.

In fact, for the first time in her entire adult life, she wants to touch a male. She wants to curl up against Selon and feel his soothing peace envelope her. She takes a small step toward him, not sure what she intends to do, maybe just unconsciously testing her resolve. Selon doesn't move, just waits patiently for her.

That's what he did on the tower, she realizes. He waited. Waited for her to talk first. Waited for her to ask questions. He never pushed, physically or verbally.

Just like all Hissa, his skin is a uniform light green, with the blue V-shaped scale pattern on his head. But unlike many of the Hissa she's met, his eyes aren't a shade of lavender or purple. If someone pressed her to name a color, she'd use the word violet. But that's not accurate either. They're violet in the middle but turn bluer toward the outside. She could easily stare at those eyes for hours, thinking about color and gentleness.

And that's really what draws her. Everything about Selon, even the color of his eyes, is the embodiment of gentleness.

Taking the last step that puts her within range, she reaches out and loosely wraps her long fingers around his muscled forearm. His eyes widen with surprise, and she can feel him tense, but he doesn't move. He remains perfectly still. She lets her hand rest there for a moment, just letting his heat seep into her cold fingers. She looks up into his face, making her eyes meet his. He's looking at her intently as if trying to read her thoughts. That makes her smile.

Good luck, she thinks, *I'm not even sure what goes on in my head half the time.*

"I want to thank you," she tells him softly with a small squeeze of her hand. "It's difficult." She stops for a moment, trying to organize all the thoughts bouncing around in her head. "I'm so happy to be with Mara, and Tiran tries to be patient, but—" She stops again, looking away. She doesn't want to say anything bad about the two. They've done so much for her and Deena. If not for Tiran and Mara, she and Deena would have died as their ship Ally fell apart around them during a raider attack.

That's one of the reasons she feels so much anxiety. She wants to make them happy, but the very fact that she has all this fear inside her makes them unhappy. Their unhappiness makes her anxious. Makes the fear worse. Makes her worse. Makes them unhappy with her.

Selon surprises her by saying, "No one would ever describe Tiran as patient. And none of them are quiet. In any way. Loyal and loving, but not patient and quiet."

Lara looks up at him and nods. "Right, yes, that's it exactly. They're happy, but noisy. It's hard."

Selon's face is sympathetic, and his hand starts to move, but he catches himself and tucks it behind his back. Lara realizes he was going to cover her hand with his and feels slightly disappointed that he didn't.

"They bang around all the time. Their sex is very loud and physical. I can hear them knocking around in their room." Lara winces a little at all the personal things she's sharing. But he doesn't look scandalized or upset. No, he nods his head encouragingly, his expression soft and amiable. "Sometimes she screams."

"She's not being abused," he's quick to assure her.

Lara frowns. "I know that." She sighs with frustration and looks down at her hand, holding onto his arm with a tight grip.

I should relax my hand, she thinks to herself. *I might be hurting him. I should let go.* She can't seem to make her hand obey.

"I know Tiran would never hurt her. It just . . ." Tears press at the back of her eyes, and Selon makes a small sound. She looks up at his face. His expression is full of compassion.

"It just makes you remember things," he states, his words barely a whisper now. He pulls his hand out from behind his back and slowly moves it toward the hand clutching his forearm. He lets his hand hover over hers for several long seconds, and Lara realizes he's giving her time to protest. Time to pull away.

She barely knows this Hissa, but it's the little things like giving her time to say no to a touch that makes her want to tell him everything. To open up her chest and pour out all the words she can't seem to say to anyone else.

To show how much she trusts him, both to him and to herself, she moves her free hand over his. Then she presses it down so his right hand is captured between hers.

The contact seems to help center her, and she takes a deep breath, feeling the tears recede. She's not sure why, but the heat of Selon's hand warming the back of one hand and the palm of the other, starts to make her feel warm all over her body. She likes the feeling and closes her eyes to enjoy it.

His hand wiggles slightly, and she fights the feeling of disappointment at the thought he wants to end the contact. Without opening her eyes, determined to relish his touch until it's completely over, she lifts her left hand off his. But he doesn't pull away. He flips his hand over and weaves his four fingers into her five digits.

She gives a little gasp, and her eyes fly open to look first at their interlocked fingers, then at his face. She doesn't see anything there but kindness and a hint of fear. She doesn't feel an instinctual need to jerk away. Experimentally, she moves her hand in his, feeling his large fingers sliding against hers. He's all muscles and strength, and yet he doesn't grasp her too tightly or overwhelm her.

They stand there, holding hands. He doesn't push for more, and she doesn't pull away. This feels so unexpectedly normal that it makes her marvel. Not even Tiran tries to touch her. He knows better. Everyone knows better. Even those that get too close and send her into a panic attack know not to make physical contact.

But her fear of being touched is nowhere to be seen at the moment. Right now, she's entranced by this Hissa.

"I hope I'm not keeping you from doing anything important," she murmurs.

"I finished my assignment on the moon," he tells her after a moment's hesitation. There's something he's not telling her, but she doesn't push. She's going to give him the same courtesy he's giving her. Let him tell her everything in his own time.

"I'm glad," she says.

"I don't know anything about this," he points out, nodding his head toward the shuttle.

"You don't need to," she assures him. It's nice to be the one who can be confident for once. "Engines and ships are easy. They tell you what's wrong. Sometimes what's wrong is complicated and requires a lot of diagnostics, but it's always findable. And fixable." What she doesn't need to say is that there are a lot of other things that aren't as straightforward as mechanics. But Selon understands. Intuitively, she knows he understands what she's not saying. She doesn't need to explain further. That's part of why she feels so much trust so quickly.

When they were on the roof of the com tower together, he looked so uncomfortable at first. He moved as if he'd never been up there before. She has no doubt he does like climbing, but she'd eat an engine regorge valve if he spoke the truth when he said he climbed up on the tower regularly.

No, it was obvious he was up there because of her. Any other Hissa would've pushed her to get down, alerted the authorities, or used the situation to get close to her. Selon did none of those things. He just hung out with her.

She can't remember ever being so relaxed in a male's company.

What strikes her as mildly amusing is the fact that he isn't small. By Hissa standards, standing only six and a half feet tall, Tiran is considered rather short. But Selon, just like many of the men assigned to guard her, stands slightly taller than average. He's also incredibly broad. Even covered in clothing, it's easy to see how muscular his shoulders, torso, and arms are. His hand practically engulfs hers.

Staring at their hands, she checks in with her anxiety and finds no impulse to run and hide. No intense drive to pull away. There's only a hyper-awareness of Selon, but not in a bad way. She can smell his scent, pleasant and masculine. The warmth from his body radiating next to her.

Is this what it's like to be normal? To be aware of a male as something desirable instead of something fearful?

That thought is so shocking she tugs her hand out of his. He lets go the moment she moves and puts both his hands behind his back and takes a small step away from her.

"Panels," she blurts out. "I need to finish pulling panels. And I want to take apart the steering gimbles and . . ." Her sentence trails off as she looks back at the shuttle.

"Just tell me how I can help," Selon offers. "Or I can go sit over there." He holds up a data pad. "I've got plenty here to keep me entertained so you won't hurt my feelings if you tell me to stay out of your way."

"Yes, that's a good idea. You go sit. I'll tell you if I need any help," she says, relieved that once again he knows exactly what to say to put her at ease.

Without another word, he settles himself on one of the large chairs that take up a corner of the bay. Along with the chairs are a table, a cot, and piles of packages. She's sure they're food and clothing. For some reason, the Hissa don't think the Decanted women can go anywhere without extra food and clothing on hand.

Well, this time they might be right. She's going to ruin these clothes as she works. Whistling cheerfully to herself, she starts pulling panels off again.

She's never been so gleeful to get dirty.

CHAPTER

6

The days go by quickly, and they are some of the happiest Lara's experienced in a long time. Every morning, Selon arrives bright and early to escort her to the repair bay. He stays with her all day, either helping, or sitting in the corner and working on his data pad. Occasionally the data pad will start beeping, and he'll step outside to have a conversation with someone. But other than that, he never moves or makes a sound unless she asks.

She starts all their conversations. If she doesn't initiate, he doesn't come anywhere near her. It's her little slice of paradise. No other males. No pushy guards. No crowds. Just her, a shuttle in need of an overhaul, and Selon.

And today the boosters are supposed to arrive. She's finished prepping most of the shuttle and getting the booster mounts installed. She's excited about their arrival but also a little sad. She'll be done with this project within a day, two at the max once she has the boosters. She doesn't want to be done. She doesn't want her time in the repair bay with Selon to be over.

Her biggest hope is that the Hissa Council will be so impressed with the booster assembly that they'll ask her to do all their cargo shuttles. That would be months of work. Months!

The thought makes her giddy.

"I finished cleaning this. Where do you want me to put it?" Selon asks, effortlessly holding a very heavy engine nozzle. What would it be like to be so strong?

"Right there," she says, pointing to her feet. "There are still a few things I want to do before we put it back on." He carefully sets the nozzle down where she indicates and without another word, heads back to his corner.

"Do you remember what it was like?" she asks, stopping his movement.

"Remember what?" he asks, turning back around to face her.

"Before the Great Death. Do you remember the female Hissa? Your mom?"

"I do," he responds easily, with no hesitation. "I had a mother and two sisters. I was old enough to form good memories before they passed. My mother was a strong Hissa woman. She was a high-ranking officer in the Hissa military. Both my sisters were older than I. Tuyan, the oldest, was learning to be an engineer, but with biosystems. My other sister, Sulin, wanted to be like our mother."

"What was it like to be the youngest?" she finds herself asking. She and Mara never had a mother or father. Never had a family except for each other. Honestly, that was more than most Decanted children had. But that doesn't make her any less envious of those who got to have families growing up.

"Both wonderful and horrible," he answers with one of his trademark smiles. Stepping to the side, he leans against the shuttle and tucks his hands in the pockets of his pants. His eyes go unfocused as he loses himself in memories. "Sulin loved to tease me because I liked reading so much. She would badger me until I played with her. She was competitive, so she would routinely trounce me at any games we played. Tuyan was quiet, introspective. And very studious. Sulin wasn't good at being still, but Tuyan could lose herself in her school assignments for hours. Sometimes our parents would have to remind her to eat. All three of them, my sisters and my mother, were all very special people. There isn't a day that goes by that I don't miss them." His words are full of longing and loss.

"What about your father?" she asks gently.

"I lost him as well," Selon admits. "But not from the disease directly. After my oldest sister died, his heart was broken. She held on the longest, and we'd both hoped she might survive, despite all evidence to the contrary. Once she was gone, he felt he had no reason to live."

"But he had you," she protests. "You were just a child. He still needed to care for you."

"He did love me, but he was too grief-stricken to think clearly. He ended his life with one of my mother's old service weapons. I heard the discharge and knew what it meant. I didn't even go to check. I just left the house and moved in with my friend's family. We all grieved together. That was one of the costs of the disease. We didn't just lose people who got sick, we lost people who weren't even infected. So many men ended their own lives because they couldn't live beyond the loss of their families. Many cite the statistic that we lost half our male population to the disease. That's not entirely accurate. We lost about a quarter of our males to the disease and another quarter to suicide. That's why I dedicated my life—"

He abruptly stops talking, and for the first time since she met him on top of the tower, he looks flummoxed. Tense and uncomfortable, he pulls his hands out of his pockets and rubs them over his face and smooth head.

She has the strongest urge to step forward, not because she wants comfort, but because she wants to give comfort. She takes half a step toward him, only to have a loud bang come from the front of the bay, causing her to gasp and jump back.

No one's come near the bay the entire time they've been there. She's seen almost no one on their commutes back and forth. For a time, she forgot there's an entire planet out there. That noise is an unwelcome reminder.

"Lara Stray?" An unfamiliar male voice calls out her name.

The voice is excited, eager, and utterly destroys the calm serenity of the bay for her. Fear invades her, and she moves on instinct. Scampering away from the unknown voice, she leaps onto the engine mount behind her. In seconds, she's clambered to the top of the cargo shuttle, flattening herself out and shoving her hand in her mouth to keep from making a sound.

"Hello?" the voice calls out again. "Lara? I have the boosters here!"

"Just leave them," Selon calls back, and Lara's surprised at his unfriendly gruff tone. She's never heard him be anything other than gracious and amiable. But, then again, no one's ever intruded on them before. He promised he'd keep people away, and he might be feeling disagreeable that someone dared enter the bay.

"Sure. Do you know how to operate an ambulatory stand? They're too heavy to lift by yourself if you accidentally dump them off. I should walk it in for you."

"I'm sure it's fine," Selon replies, and Lara can hear impatience in his voice.

"Let me just walk it in for you," the other man insists, and his voice is closer now.

Lara squeezes her eyes shut. She can handle being in the presence of strange men, but not when she's given no time to prepare. The male's sudden appearance feels like an invasion. An attack.

"Set down the control and walk away," Selon growls loud enough for Lara to hear.

"I just want to—" the other male starts to say, and then she hears Selon moving. There's no sound of a scuffle, but she can hear talking in low intense tones. She knows this stranger wants to meet her. To at least see her. She understands the Hissa are desperate for women. Desperate for someone to love, mate with, and to bear them children. None of them would deliberately hurt her. But knowing those facts doesn't stop the deep fear from rising up in her chest.

Fear of being pinned against a wall. Fear of being forced. Fear of being helpless.

She hears the man leave, and then it's quiet in the bay again. She stays still, trying to slow her breathing like Deena taught her.

"He's gone," Selon calls out. "You don't need to come down. Stay up there as long as you wish. There's no rush to do anything."

His deep voice does wonderful things to her. His words ease the constriction in her chest, and she's able to take her fist out of her mouth and take a full, deep breath. "Please keep talking," she says and isn't surprised when her voice comes out raspy. Sudden panic does that to her.

"You're safe," he tells her. His voice is moving, and she wonders where he's going. "It's just you and me in the bay now. No one else. I closed and locked the bay door and requested guards posted outside. No more surprise guests, I promise. And the guards will remain outside also. It will only be you and me in here. Or only you. I can leave also if you wish."

His voice sounds muffled now. Is he in the shuttle? Then a

hatch on the roof opens just an inch or so, and she can see Selon peering out. "When you're ready," he tells her, keeping the hatch mostly closed, "you can come back down this way."

She nods at him, slowly uncurling her body and sliding toward the hatch. She pushes it all the way open, and Selon turns to move out of her way so she can make her way down, but that's not what she wants. She wants to feel the same thing she felt earlier.

One of his hands is resting on the hatch opening, and she snatches it with both her hands and draws it in toward her chest. With a tight hold on his limb, she curls her body around his arm and rests her forehead on the warm flesh at the crook of his elbow. Eyes closed, she breathes the scent of him in through her nose, letting it soothe her.

He stands still, but stiff. His hand lies unmoving in her grip, the muscles of his arm tense against her cheek. "Lara?"

She can't explain her impulse to him. All she can do is whisper one word. "Please."

The fear that pushed her to flee is starting to fade. Her heartbeat is calming, and her chest doesn't feel so constricted. Hugging his hand and forearm to her chest makes her feel like she's got a solid hold in the world. Something to grasp to keep from being overwhelmed.

He gives a small sound of distress, and Lara opens her eyes and realizes that by grabbing his arm, she's twisted him at an odd angle, forcing him to bend almost backward so she doesn't tear something in his shoulder. He could easily pull out of her grip, but instead he's balancing himself in the hatch and trying to remain still despite his obvious discomfort.

She immediately lets go of his arm. She sees disappointment in his face as she straightens up. He's about to say something when she grabs the top of his shirt, braces her feet on the lip of the hatch, and drags him out onto the top of the shuttle. The shirt rips a little but holds enough so she can use the brute strength gifted to her by the Decanted technology.

It's the boldest thing she's ever done, but it doesn't even register. She's much too focused on getting ahold of him again to care that she just manhandled a male so much bigger than herself. His touch has a calming power, and there's a lot she's willing to do to get that feeling back. To regain that sense of tranquility again. For a brief moment, her mind wasn't warring with her. Wasn't pushing her to run, hide, cry, or panic. Her mind was blessedly quiet.

Because of him.

He gives a little gasp of surprise and flails for just a moment and then finds his balance on the almost flat roof of the shuttle. Lara waits impatiently for him to sit up, and as soon as he doesn't need his hand to keep from sliding around, she grabs it again, curling herself around him and giving a sigh of contentment.

Yes, this is perfect.

CHAPTER

7

Selon keeps himself still and tries to get his confused thoughts and impulses into some kind of order. Peaceful and happy, Lara lies next to him, curled around his arm, making contented noises. He takes a deep breath through his nose and is relieved when he doesn't smell the acrid scent of her fear. The harsh scent of her fear hit him hard when he first opened the hatch, and it took all his willpower not to hurry to her and gather her up in his arms in an attempt to comfort her.

With his free hand, he feels the tear at the top of his shirt. The clothing he wears might not be as durable as what the miners use, but it's not something soft and diaphanous like what a Hissa female traditionally wore. When she grabbed him and pulled him out of the hatch, his brain froze. Her movements were so fast and incredibly strong that he wondered briefly if she didn't have some kind of telekinetic power. He lets his hand drop away from the top of his torn garment.

"You're very strong," he murmurs and hears her give a muffled giggle. She hugs his arm tighter to her chest, lacing her fingers into his again. He's careful to keep just enough tension in his fingers to return the embrace without overwhelming her. The last thing he wants to do is make her feel trapped.

"You don't need to move, but may I lie down too?" Selon asks. He can feel his body wanting to slide off the slick surface of the shuttle. If he's able to spread his length along the top, hopefully he'll stop the sliding.

"Yes," she says simply and scoots a little to give him some room. He ends up lying down with one foot hooked in the open hatch and his upper body curled around Lara. He's close enough to feel her warmth but careful not to make contact. He's not touching her with anything but the arm she's curled around.

She gives a small sigh and moves enough to let her back touch his front, then settles back down again. Her touch is innocent but causes a problematic chain reaction within him. He wants to reach over with his other arm and nestle her in, closer to his body. But he manages to resist the urge and turns his focus to his breathing. He needs to calm the emotions rioting through his body.

He almost attacked the male who brought the boosters. The male just wanted to meet Lara and begged Selon to give her a gift from him. If anyone understands the desperation of the Hissa men, it's him. He's spent most of the last few years keeping men from killing themselves. Hopelessness and depression are running rampant among the Hissa. There are even days when Selon and others in his profession are close to succumbing also. Falling into a pit of despair and looking for ways to end their own lives, rather than face a future devoid of companionship and children. But just like the rest of Hissa, Selon keeps trying as best he can to counsel, console, and guide everyone else.

He wonders for a moment if he isn't taking advantage of Lara.

She's suffered intense trauma in her past and is now vulnerable. He considered his small manipulations as a necessary evil to make her feel comfortable and happy, but he ponders where the line is. How far would he go? He feels the same drive to find a mate as all the other men. The only difference is his extensive training in emotional control. Who is to say he isn't using that control to lure Lara to him now? He might need to talk to one of his colleagues.

"Deena had a guy she liked to use for sex when she was in heat." Lara suddenly starts talking, drawing Selon out of his thoughts. He's now familiar with her habit of randomly starting a conversation, so it doesn't confuse him. As usual, he responds to her seemingly non-sequitur comment with a question.

"Heat?"

"Yeah, Deena goes into heat when she ovulates. She was bought as a wife for an old rich guy. When she was ordered, the buyer specified that it needed to be obvious when she was fertile and that she'd crave a male. I guess it was to ensure children." As curious as he is about Deena, he doesn't ask any further questions regarding the pilot. Instead, he nudges Lara along in her story.

"Was the guy there only to provide sex for Deena?"

"No, he was pretty good with the navigation system too." She pauses for a moment then adds, "And he'd cook. We both liked some of the stuff he cooked. Anyway, Deena only wanted him for those few days and had no interest in sex the rest of the month. So, he started looking for me one day. I guess he was horny. He had me cornered in the machine room, and she walked in."

"Was Deena angry?"

"Furious, but not at me. She was angry at the guy. She hurt him. Grabbed my long gauge trans-line balancer and hit him upside the head. Knocked him out. Then we dragged him to his bunk, and she confined him to quarters. She tossed him off at the next station. She never brought another guy on board after that. She kept me safe."

Ah, there's the reason for the story. She's showing him not only her deep affection for Deena, but also her insecurities. When they first started working together, she probably assumed that at some point Deena would pick her comfort over Lara's health and happiness. Then Deena chose Lara's safety before anything else, earning Lara's eternal love and gratitude.

"What did she do about it? About going into heat with no male onboard?"

"Drugs," Lara explains succinctly. "She drugs herself for a few days and just suffers through."

"She's a good friend."

"She's my family."

"But she isn't your only family," Selon points out. Lara becomes quiet. The silence lasts so long he might have thought she'd fallen asleep, except her thumb is rubbing along the side of his hand.

"I love Mara," she finally states. "But it's been a long time since we were slaves together. I'm scared she'll get tired of dealing with me. Deena knows me and still loves me. Mara doesn't know me anymore."

"You need to give Mara a chance to get to know you," Selon urges her gently. "She's never stopped looking for you."

"And she's got Tiran now." Lara gives a resigned sigh that breaks Selon's heart. "She'll probably start having kids soon. I'm not sure I should be near them as they grow. I'm too broken to be around children."

"You think you might hurt them?" Selon asks, letting the surprise he feels show.

"No, but I can't protect them. I can't do anything but run and hide when I'm scared. And everything scares me," she admits with another sigh. "I wish I was a warrior like Mara, but I'm not. I've never been. But now, I'm also frightened on top of not being able to fight. I'm worse than useless because I might do something unpredictable and dangerous during an attack."

"You're not scared now," Selon points out, flexing his captured hand just a little to make his point. She makes a small sound and tightens herself around his arm for a moment, giving him a kind of hug.

"You're different," she tells him, and Selon feels his heartbeat speed up a little and his skin get warm. "I don't know why, but I feel better around you. You're just . . ." She searches for a word, then turns her head so she can look at him over her shoulder, her deep gold eyes are open and guileless. "You make me feel peaceful. Whole. Like everything's going to be fine. And you smell really good. I don't know how to describe it, but it's comforting."

"I'm glad," Selon manages to choke out. Her words are affecting his body in ways he didn't expect, and he hopes fervently she doesn't notice the erection suddenly straining the front of his pants. Before he can get his overheated brain to think of anything else to say, a bell sounds in the bay, and Lara tenses for a second but doesn't move.

"It's the bay door. Someone is asking for entrance," Selon explains. "Don't be alarmed. There are guards posted at the entrance now. No one can just walk in." He brings up his free hand with the data bracelet to see what's going on. "It's food."

Lara sits up and releases his arm with a small smile. "Great! I didn't eat this morning. I'm starving!"

The change in her might be startling for someone who hasn't witnessed her go through a panic attack. But over the last few days, Selon's gotten firsthand experience of her milder anxiety attacks and one full-blown panic attack. He knows that after she recovers from an anxiety attack, she desperately wants to pretend it never happened. To that end, the moment she feels steady at all, she wants to jump up and resume whatever she was doing before the attack.

That's assuming the anxiety attack doesn't evolve into a full-blown panic attack with a corresponding spike of adrenaline. The strange biology of these Decanted twins means that after the high of an adrenaline rush, they crash quickly and hard, requiring hours of slumber before they can function again. That happened the second day at the repair bay. An incoming shuttle's engine failed, and it crashed at the far end of the port. No one was seriously injured, but the crash was loud and shocking, causing Lara to succumb to a panic attack.

In her panic, she managed to curl herself into an engine discharge port. It took a lot of gentle persuasion, but she finally calmed enough to climb out and cling to Selon. When the panic subsided, her eyelids got heavy, and she started swaying on her feet.

Prepared for this, Selon guided her toward a cot in the corner of the bay. He made her comfortable, and when she woke up several hours later, he let her resume work without comment.

At the time, he wanted to talk to her about the panic attack and her reaction, but he didn't. Instead, he just let her chatter about different kinds of fuel mixing mechanisms. His job is to let her talk at her own pace. The Council might be pressuring him to fix her as if she's some kind of machine, but everyone knows very well that there's no timeline to this kind of healing.

He was rewarded later for his patience when she explained sharp, unexpected noises are one of her triggers. It reminds her of a ship being fired on. The raider ship where she was held captive was in numerous battles and was constantly taking damage. She was never sure if that battle was going to be her last or not. And sometimes she wasn't sure if she cared.

As far as he is concerned, that conversation was one of the biggest steps they've taken so far in her healing process. She's growing so confident in their relationship that she's willing to share sensitive memories. With all this progress, he doesn't want to cause a setback by displaying anything she might construe as a sexual advance.

To that end, he maneuvers himself carefully, trying to keep his erection from her line of sight. He stumbles down the hatch and hears her give a little cry of alarm. "Are you okay, Selon?" she calls to him as she gracefully climbs down after him.

"I'm perfectly fine," he assures with a quick grin. "We can't all be fast, agile, and strong like you."

"I'm sure you're stronger than I am," she tells him with an

answering grin as they make their way out of the shuttle.

"But nowhere near as fast," he confesses without shame. "I heard your sister beat Woken in hand-to-hand combat. I thought he let her win. Now I'm starting to understand how she might have bested him. Speed can trump size in a lot of ways."

Lara's smile widens a little. "I've met Woken. He's a giant. But Mara's a good fighter. She trained very hard when we were owned. I wish I could've seen the fight."

Selon allows her to jump down from the shuttle without offering to lift her. She lands with ease next to him, so close she's almost touching him. Her smell wafts up to his nose, and the erection he finally got under control threatens to rise again.

He turns abruptly. "I'll get the food." He sees her give him a startled look before he strides off.

At the smaller bay door, he finds several males holding platters overflowing with food. He frowns, first at the food, then at the three eager faces pleading with him. Normally, the food is left on a service cart for him to wheel inside. This is not standard procedure.

"We have food for Lara," one says, holding up his platter.

"All made from the freshest ingredients. I grew some in my garden," another one declares proudly.

"I made this one with Dolean spices in it!" the third announces. "I got a tin last year, and I've been saving it for a special occasion. I'd like to present it to her. I know she's fearful. I'll keep my distance. I won't touch her. I'll just present her with the food and speak my intentions."

All three nod their heads enthusiastically. Even though all three have broken protocol, Selon feels sympathy. With a heavy heart, he shakes his head. "A male already scared her earlier when he brought the engines. She climbed to the top of the shuttle, crying and hiding. I'm afraid three males presenting her with food would be too much."

"Who scared her?" one of the guards asks, his gruff voice angry.

"It was an accident. But to avoid any other accidents, you're now here," Selon tells the guard quickly and then turns his attention back to the other three. "Let's compromise. Do any of you have memory paper handy? You can write what you would like to say, and I'll take it to her with the food."

The three set down their platters and start searching frantically for memory paper. One of them has an entire roll and rips three sheets off to give to the other two. They speak to their papers and the words form in neat lines across the gray surface. Each one carefully tucks the paper onto their platter and Selon finds himself trying to juggle three large platters of food as they are picked up and thrust at him.

"Don't drop them!" one of the males begs. "Or at least don't drop mine!"

Another male growls. "Don't drop mine either."

All three males are looking at each other with building fury, and Selon retreats into the bay while the guard sends the men away. Selon shakes his head with frustration. Either Lara's going to need to find a mate soon, or they might need to take her off-planet until she's ready to pick one.

Halfway across the bay, Lara rushes up to take one of the platters from him, her eyes wide, "This is a lot of food for just the two of us."

"I think it's all meant just for you," Selon points out with a small grin. "They left you notes."

Lara picks a clear piece of floor under the front of the shuttle to place her platter and then sits down cross-legged. She plucks out one of the notes and starts reading it, but frowns.

She hands it to him. "It's in Hissa."

Selon scans the note. "This male's name is Legan, and he works at the city center for the Council. He states he has a nice house, he's healthy, and he did well in last year's competitions."

Lara holds up her hand to stop him. "Let me guess the rest. He wants to buy me beautiful clothes. I'll never have to work. Our children will be treasured, and he has all his mother's jewels to give me."

"Not in that order, but yes," Selon confirms, and watches Lara's shoulders slump a little. "I take it you've gotten a lot of these?"

"Constantly. Things are always arriving at Tiran's door addressed to me. There are usually gifts too. Even a pair of Dovi birds. I was going to set them free. I hate seeing things in cages, but Tiran told me they don't survive in the wild, so he gave them to Penon."

She's quiet for a moment, nibbling on some of the food. Selon sets the note down and starts eating. As is their pattern, he remains quiet and lets her decide how much or little she wishes to talk.

"It doesn't help that Tiran and Mara argue all the time on what to do with me," Lara states with a sad little frown. "Mara wants to take me and Deena on Witch and travel. Tiran wants all of us to stay here. Well, maybe not Deena. She really annoys him. I don't think he'd mind if she ended up off-planet." They both chuckle at that.

"Do you ever say anything about what you want while this is going on?"

"I try, but when they all look at me, I freeze up," she confesses. "Especially when Tiran's looking at me."

"Maybe you just need to practice," Selon suggests. He picks up a piece of food from one of the platters and pops it in his mouth. The Dolean spices explode across his tongue, and he almost groans. "And you need to eat some of this." Without thinking, he picks up another piece and holds it out to her. She stares at his hand for a moment, as if debating, then leans forward and eats the bite from his fingers.

Her delicate mouth barely touches him, but it's enough to send a shock of desire through him. The intimacy of her lips brushing along his fingertips makes his unruly dick come right back to life.

At this rate, all she'll need to do is brush past me in a corridor and I'll spill my seed right in my pants, he thinks sourly to himself.

"That's very good," she murmurs after eating her bite. She takes another from the same tray. "How do I practice talking to Tiran without Tiran?" she asks, then pops the bite into her mouth.

"You just practice with me," Selon explains simply.

Lara shakes her head. "That won't work. You don't scare me."

Selon makes a small, happy sound. "Thank you for the compliment. But I don't need to be scary. We just practice the words until you can say them automatically. Later, it will get easier to get the words out without needing to practice."

She smiles at him. "It's like the wiring on Ally." At his blank look, her smile widens. "I had to reference the schematics a lot at first, but I started remembering it and eventually only had to look at the schematics occasionally."

"I guess that's a fair analogy. Let's try it then." Selon straightens up and gives Lara a mock glare. "I say she stays right here!" She giggles at his bad impression of Tiran's thick Space Standard accent. She doesn't say anything, and finally Selon drops the glare and leans forward a bit. "It's your turn. Demand something, anything. Just give it a try."

She nibbles on her lip nervously, the food in her fingers forgotten as she thinks. Finally, she takes a deep breath and speaks.

All her words come out of her mouth so rapidly that the sentence almost sounds like one long word.

"I-want-my-own-place-to-live-in-and-a-shop-of-my-own-to-fix-things."

Selon can't help the startled expression that crosses his face. "You want to live alone? On Hissa?"

Lara looks away, her face full of worry. She sets the food back on the platter and draws her knees up to her chest and wraps her arms around her shins.

"I know it's too dangerous to live alone, but I'm tired of being so close to other people. I've never lived like this. Even when the captain owned me I . . ." She pauses, still refusing to meet his eyes. "I was mostly left alone as long as I stayed out of sight. I can't get out of sight here. I'm always watched. Always surrounded. There's no humming engine or ratcheting bio-cycler to make noise for me. No tucked away place in the maintenance corridors or old pipe routing room for me to set up a cot and sleep. No place to be alone."

Her admission makes Selon feel like he finally understands one of the reasons Lara is struggling. Hissa might be too peaceful for her. She's never experienced quiet in her adult life. The loud sounds coming from engines and ships systems comforted her. The cramped spaces she created made her feel safe and secure. They might have taken her out of danger, but her mind, so used to certain conditions, keeps telling her she isn't safe. Keeps urging her to find a place that will make her feel safe again.

He's sure being surrounded by desperate, lonely males isn't helping either.

"That's a good start," he tells her, and she looks up at him with a small smile.

"Really? I thought you might think I'm an idiot for wanting those things."

"Never," Selon assures her, and then gives her a smile of his own. "I hate flying," he confesses. "I get sick to my stomach every time." He reaches into his pocket and pulls out a small chunk of metal on a cord and hands it to her. "After she entered a Family Pact with my father, my mother left the military to become a thermal mapper here on Hissa. She found that deep in a cave. She drilled a hole, put it on a necklace and wore it all her life. Dad tried to give her all kinds of prettier things, but she refused. She said it was a piece of fallen star waiting millions of years for her to find it. When she died, I started carrying it around with me. I can't fly if I don't have it with me."

Lara gently strokes the smooth stone and then hands it back. "That's lovely."

Selon nods and tucks it back into his pants. "I've never told anyone about it because I worry they will think I'm weak. We all have things we keep secret, Lara. The truth is they're rarely as bad as we think they are."

She dips her head, so her hair covers her face again. He's not sure what she's thinking and fights the impulse to ask.

"I'm full," she states abruptly and jumps up. "I want to finish prepping the booster to be mounted. That way I can start attaching them first thing tomorrow."

Cursing himself silently for pushing too hard, Selon gets up and follows her to the back of the shuttle. "Right. Back to work," he mutters.

CHAPTER

8

It's late when Selon starts making noises about her stopping for the day, causing her to frown. That makes him relent and offer her an alternative: take a break for dinner then continue afterward for as long as she wishes. That makes her smile and readily agree. And that's what makes Selon so perfect. He never demands. Never frowns, growls, glowers, or argues. He just talks in a soft, reasonable voice. When she doesn't want something, he doesn't automatically overrule her, he discusses it with her. He is so different from Tiran. He's different from every other Hissa she's interacted with.

This means that by the time Lara's ready to stop for the day, it's dark outside, and Diminish, the smaller of Hissa's two moons, has risen high in the sky.

"This is a good time to quit," she says, tucking away the tools she's stored in her coveralls for quick access while she was putting the delicate sensor node on the engine back together.

"Thank the moons," Selon says cheerfully, rubbing hands over his face. Immediately she feels guilty.

"I'm sorry. You must be exhausted," she murmurs. She's not sure what time it is, but she looks up to see Diminish clearly in the skylight of the hangar, which tells her it's very late at night. But her worry evaporates when Selon chuckles.

"I'm not that fatigued, but I'll admit I'm not looking forward to dealing with the sensor node on the second engine. I don't know if you realize this, but we worked on that for most of the day. I think my eyes have crossed from trying to distinguish all the small parts you wanted me to deal with!"

"Maybe I should get you a set of digital eye assistance viewers," she teases, enjoying this banter. The only person she's ever bantered with as an adult is Deena. Talking to Selon with this level of ease is a new and enjoyable experience. "They make a few kinds that are light and perch right on your nose."

"Digital eye assistance viewers?" he repeats with a shake of his head. "I'm not quite that old yet. But perhaps I will be by the time we're done here!"

"Oh no, I promise the rest will go quickly," she assures him, still grinning. He reaches to put a few tools sitting on the ground under the engine away when she waves him off with a hand. "Don't bother with those. I'll need them right away when we start up again tomorrow."

"Maybe we can sleep in a bit?" Selon asks tentatively, and that makes Lara frown and examine his face. She's started feeling so comfortable with this Hissa that she's taken to tying her hair up and meeting his eyes more often than not.

It's strange for her to realize that not only does she not fear this male, but the idea of spending less time in his presence bothers her. Sleeping in late would deprive her of time with him.

"Do you need more sleep?" she questions carefully.

"No, but you must," he answers easily. Relief fills her.

"If that's your concern then don't worry," she says quickly. "I need very little sleep, and honestly I don't sleep well at Tiran's house so being here is a big relief." Selon doesn't frown at her words, but he does seem thoughtful.

"Tomorrow, can we talk about how you could be made more comfortable?" he requests. She loves the way he asks things. He never demands she answer right away. Often his questions are open-ended so she can decide when she'll answer them, if ever. To her surprise, she's found herself telling him more about her time with the raiders than she's even confided in Deena. Only bits and pieces, but it's given her more and more courage as the days have passed.

Of course, Deena's never really told her much about her past either, but Selon is an open book to any inquiry she makes. That makes her feel like they're on a more equal footing, that it's not just her baring her soul, but both of them exploring their pasts and present.

With everything put away, they head to the front of the repair bay. The massive doors used to move the cargo shuttles in and out are shut and locked tight, but the smaller pass-through door is cracked open.

"Are you hungry? We could pick up something at the automated kiosk in the town square on our way to Tiran's house," Selon offers as he pushes the door fully open. Before she can answer him, a wave of movement and sound hits her as a mass of Hissa men surge forward.

Lara shrinks back with a gasp as hundreds of voices all call for her attention at once. The guards are trying to push the men back, but it's two against hundreds. Even with armor and loaded with effective non-lethal weapons, they can do little against so many.

She looks around wildly and turns to see Selon only a stride away, grasping the door in shock at the sight of all the men. Without another thought, she ducks behind him and clambers onto his back, wrapping her legs around his waist and snaking her hands under his armpits and up to grasp the front of his shoulders. She buries her face in his back and gives a panicked sob.

She can feel Selon's body tense at her sudden actions, but he doesn't try and touch her with his hands, and he doesn't pull her off. Instead, he backs up until they are within the safety of the bay and the door is shut and securely locked.

"I don't mind you being my backpack," he tells her gently. "But you can't hang onto me like that forever."

"That's what you think," she mutters into his back. She feels safe and comfortable clinging to him and is reluctant to get down. He doesn't seem to be bothered by her weight and contact with him is keeping her looming panic attack at bay.

She loosens her legs enough so she can pull herself up a little higher, then re-wraps her legs just above his hips. He gives a startled grunt, but other than that makes no move to talk her down or force her off his back. Now she's in a position to pull herself up and peek over his shoulder if she wants to. "I'm comfortable," she tells him simply.

He remains quiet for a moment and then gives a little sigh. She hopes it's not because she's frustrating him. "It seems we might be trapped," he finally admits. "I don't know why so many men have gone against Council decree and gathered here, but I'm sure it will be a while before they disperse."

Lara tightens her grip with a little excitement. "We could sleep here for the night."

"Here?" Selon doesn't sound thrilled with the prospect, making Lara stifle a laugh.

"The seats along each side of the shuttle cabin fold down to make beds. And the shuttle has basic elimination and bathing facilities." Lara can't help the excitement in her voice. "It'll be like the old days when Deena and I first started. We worked for a couple of companies that used similar shuttles. Not as nice or new but same basic design."

"So, you want to spend the night in a shuttle?" Selon's voice isn't derisive or sarcastic, but simply interested.

"The bay doors might be locked, but there are a lot of men out there, and these bays aren't built to withstand a siege. On the other hand, the shuttle doors lock," Lara explains quickly, hoping he will agree to her plan. "I can make it so that the shuttle doors won't open from the outside. That's easy. And these shuttles can handle a grade four impact, so unless those guys know how to use a plasma torch and have a months' worth of patience, they aren't getting in once I lock us down."

Selon turns and regards the large shuttle taking up most of the repair bay. "It's going to get hot and stuffy in there without the engines to run the life support," he mentions hesitantly. She can feel he's caving and presses her advantage.

"I can hook the shuttle to shore power. Give me thirty seconds, and I can get the systems on. Easy as pulling a termiarian out of a cooling port!" She wiggles on his back a little from the excitement. The ship might not be in the air or out in space, but it will still feel like home.

"Do termiarians get into cooling ports often?" Selon asks, and Lara gives a small laugh.

"Every time we landed at Goover station I'd have to clean them out," she says with an enthusiastic nod, then waits quietly for Selon to respond. She nuzzles her cheek against his back, ignoring the protest from her hands forced into the same position for so long. Because she's Decanted, her sense of smell is better than the average human, but still nowhere near as good as a Hissa's. But even with her less acute sense of smell, their close proximity inundates her with his scent. Just like the rest of him, his smell is perfect.

She wonders if she can talk him into sharing a bunk with her. She isn't sure what she wants, except she knows she doesn't want to let go. Contact with his body feels as important to her as her next breath.

"Let's contact Mara and Tiran," Selon says, finally striding toward the back of the bay where the communication equipment is mounted on a wall. He carries her weight easily, and soon he's activating the display, and Mara and Tiran appear.

"I just got word the port is mobbed," Tiran growls. "I didn't think of the danger, but shift change for Diminish happened today. That's almost a thousand males who just arrived back on the planet after being stationed on the moon for the last three months. They got off the transport shuttle and refused to leave the port until Lara was presented to them. Miners are a stubborn group and prone to ignore orders if they think they know better."

"Where's Lara?" Mara searches the area around Selon anxiously for her sister. "You didn't let her out there, did you? Pienter shit! Do those men have her?"

Instead of replying, Selon turns to show them Lara clinging to his back.

Lara gives her sister a half-grin. "I'm fine."

Mara's face goes from anxiety to suspicion quickly. "Did your legs stop working?" she asks, and Tiran snickers next to her. Lara feels her face flush. Embarrassment makes her tighten her legs around Selon's waist.

"I don't mind," Selon volunteers quickly.

"I bet you don't," Deena shouts out from behind Mara. Lara can't see her in the display but grins anyway.

"I like heights," she calls back to Deena. "And he's tall, like the towers they use to dissipate heat on Fielden." She hears Deena chuckle but is surprised at the look on both Tiran's and Mara's faces. They both look upset. She feels anxiety flower inside of her again, and she quickly releases Selon, dropping to the ground. She pulls the band out of her hair and lets the shaggy mass fall into her face, hiding her features.

"I'm sorry. I didn't mean to do anything wrong," she says quickly, looking at the floor. Selon touches her shoulder, just a brush of his fingers. It's a comfort, and she wants to grab and hold his hand again but resists the urge, fearful she'll upset Mara and Tiran further.

"I think they're bothered by my actions more than yours,"

he assures her. "I know I'm not supposed to touch you, and yet it happened anyway."

"I did it. It's my fault," Lara insists, risking a glance up at the screen. "Please don't be angry at Selon. I'm the one who grabbed his hand and climbed on his back. He's kind, and he doesn't pull away or try and create more contact. Don't be angry at him."

"We aren't angry," Tiran says through clenched teeth. He's trying to control his expression and doing a very poor job. Mara pushes him until he's no longer displayed on the screen. Her face isn't angry, but she seems worried.

"It's going to be a while before we can get you home. If Selon keeps you calm, then that's great. We won't say anything if you want to touch him. Just remember, he isn't allowed to touch you. If he does, we can make sure he's kept far from you."

Lara isn't sure why it's so important that Selon not touch her. It's not as if he pushes himself on her or makes her feel threatened, but she doesn't want to question Mara and risk losing Selon, so she just nods her head quickly.

"Lara has a request," Selon says, and Lara feels her entire body lock up in fear. She glances over at him with wide eyes and takes a few quick breaths.

"I can't," she whispers to him, wrapping her arms around her waist. He leans over until his mouth is close to her ear, careful to keep his body away from her.

"You were so happy just moments ago. You want this. Just ask. I'm right here," he promises, and Lara finds his voice soothes her dread at trying to talk honestly with Mara and Tiran. She's still frightened, but it's not so bad that she can't speak. She tries to look up at the screen but can't bring herself to meet Mara's eyes. With her peripheral vision, she sees Tiran appear back on the screen.

"What would you request," he demands, his voice harsh. "I'm sure we can find a way to fulfill it."

She opens her mouth to speak, but no sound comes out. She clears her throat and glances at Selon through her hair. He's straightened back up and stands close to her without touching. His hand is right there so she grabs it and hugs it to her chest just like she did on the roof of the shuttle. She hears Mara give a little sound of surprise but ignores it and rushes to get the words out.

"I want to spend the night here. Sleep in the shuttle, here in the bay. I can convert the seats into beds, and Selon and I can spend the night."

"Was that all one word?" Tiran asks, confused. He didn't

understand her blurted Space Standard words.

She repeats herself, speaking more slowly this time. "I want to spend the night here in the bay. With Selon. In the shuttle. On the seats that fold out into beds."

Silence greets her words, and she's too afraid to look up until Deena crows with laughter. "He's cute. Ride him hard like a Pienter on Galous!"

Lara flushes but smiles, looking up in time to see Deena push her way between Tiran and Mara, knocking them both out of the picture. "It's not like that," Lara replies.

Deena rolls her eyes. "I know, but it should be! I'll smooth things over here. You have fun. Do you have food? Need anything?"

Lara shakes her head; happy her friend understands. "We have everything."

Mara tries to pull Deena out of the way, but Deena holds her off by beating her with a floppy tool used to turn food on a hot surface in the kitchen. "We won't come get you. You just wander home whenever you're ready," she calls out and then smacks something, making the feed go black. She hears Selon laughing next to her and looks up to see his amused face.

"Deena understands you," he comments.

Lara nods and smiles back at him. "We understand each other." She suddenly realizes she's still holding his hand to her chest and drops it, feeling a blush heat her face.

"I'm going to pull the beds out," she tells him and hurries off.

CHAPTER

9

Selon watches as Lara practically skips over to the open hatch of the shuttle. Her steps are light and joyful, and she even gives a little hop as she hits the ramp into the shuttle cabin. Selon wonders if he's being punished for some kind of past life transgression.

Or rewarded. It's hard to figure out which it is. He's about to share a cabin with Lara for an entire night. He'll go mad. Her smell will be all around him and he can't touch her. This is going to drive him insane.

The moons are either testing or disciplining him.
One thing she keeps doing might indicate his fortitude is being tested: she keeps touching him. Without warning, she grabs his hand and holds it to her soft chest. She wraps his arm in her embrace and he feels desire course through him. Her smell becomes devastating. He can even taste her smell on his tongue, and it's all he can do to stop himself from touching her back. Of course, there are parts of his anatomy he doesn't have that much control over. If she keeps grabbing and hugging his arm, eventually she's going to get a rude awakening when his raging erection comes into contact with her hip.

"Moons preserve me," he mutters to himself. It's been almost a year since one of the floating brothels visited Hissa, and Selon wonders if he should find a quiet place to bring himself to pleasure before the need gets too overwhelming. Before he's locked inside the small cockpit of the cargo shuttle for an entire night.

He absently looks around the bay until his eyes come to rest on the door to the bay's elimination and cleaning facilities. Maybe he can duck in there, pleasure himself, and return before Lara realizes he's missing. He's so on edge it won't take much. Before he can even move toward the far door, he hears a startled gasp and bang from inside the shuttle. He sprints under the shuttle and up the ramp, heart pounding with fear.

Inside, he finds Lara dangling from the ceiling and a broken ladder on the floor of the shuttle under her. She's kicking her legs and laughing at her predicament. He takes a moment to let the fear calm. There's no reason for him to be concerned considering she's convulsing with laughter.

"I just wanted to close the hatch," she calls down to him between fits of laughter. "And the ladder mount broke!"

Selon knows she could easily jump down after watching her feats of strength and agility over the last few days. But she doesn't. She dangles there, laughing and swinging her legs out like a child playing on a climbing structure. He grabs the ladder and tosses it out of the open hatch.

"Do you want me to catch you?" he asks, enjoying her youthful antics. He has a strong suspicion that this kind of frivolity has been a rare occurrence in her life.

"Nope!" she calls out. She swings a few times and then lets go, landing in a crouch next to him. She springs up and pats his shoulder. Her face is flushed from exertion, and her smile is wide and inviting. Selon puts both his hands behind him and locks his fingers together to keep from touching her.

"That was almost as fun as when Deena and I visited the Fielden's homeworld." She laughs again at some memory, and to Selon's surprise, she rests her hand on his shoulder, leaving it there as she talks.

"They have this massive planet-wide party every few years, and we were delivering supplies and got invited to stay. Fieldens are humanoid in shape, but not interested in human females at all. Deena and I had the best time. I even won one of the games, and they gave me this big box of unrecognizable stuff. Turns out it's their version of chocolate. We couldn't eat it, but I was able to trade it for parts."

Selon wants to encourage her to talk, ask her questions, do what he's trained to do, but his mind has seized up. No words form in his brain and travel to his mouth. Nothing. All he can do is feel her hand resting on his shoulder. He realizes he's staring at it when she draws her hand away from him, her smile dimming slightly.

He was too busy being worried about her panicking earlier to enjoy their close contact. But now she's touching him again, voluntarily. It's almost too much.

I'm failing, he thinks miserably. *I need to control myself and focus.*

"Deena didn't win any of the games, but she had a great time anyway." She pauses when he doesn't respond, concern causing her brows to furrow. "The expression on your face is odd. Are you tired?" she asks. "I don't know if you're used to physical labor. I mean, not to say you aren't in shape, but not all labor is the same. I could wrench on things all day but make me pilot and I get so tense I'm exhausted at the end." She's talking rapidly and Selon realizes he's just staring at her. Already the smell of her is building in the cabin, filling his nose and his lungs. He rubs his tongue on the roof of his mouth and almost groans at the taste of her there.

"Yes, tired," he manages to say. If he can just get her to lie down and be quiet, maybe he can gain some control.

"I'm sorry. It's my fault," she tells him. "Which bunk do you want?"

Selon looks away from her to see she's turned the benches on either side of the cabin into beds. They are just big enough to fit an average-sized Hissa male. He almost groans when he realizes that with the benches extended into beds, the floor space in the cabin is much smaller. There're only a few feet of walking space between the beds.

He's going to have to sleep within arm's reach of Lara. Smell her. Hear her. See her. All night.

He sits down hard on the closest bed and starts pulling off his shoes. She's already thrown blankets and pillows on the beds. He hears her move and looks up to see her shutting the hatch. She fiddles with the controls, and he hears the life support systems fire up. Crisp air fills the cabin, and he breathes in deeply, thinking to try and clear out some of Lara's tantalizing scent.

It doesn't help. He falls back on the bed with a groan, leaving his bare feet on the ground.

"You must be really tired," Lara comments as she jumps onto her bed. "You seemed fine in the hangar, but now you're falling over."

He doesn't respond. He's fighting too hard to keep himself still. He hears her rustling around, then the sound of her shoes hitting the floor. He grabs a pillow and puts it over his lap to keep from shocking her.

Patience, he tells himself. *Once she's asleep, I'll visit the shuttle bathroom and take care of my aching need.* It will be very close quarters in there, but that's still better than letting her know how much she's affecting him. The thought of causing her any fear dampens his ardor enough to risk opening his eyes and rolling his head to the side so he can see the other bed.

She stripped out of the outer garment she always wears and is now in just a short top that binds her breasts tightly and some kind of very short pants that only cover her sex. This is the first time he's seen anything but her hands and head unclothed. Her body isn't as toned as her warrior sister, Mara. She's softer and rounder with creamy white skin that he aches to touch. This is by far the more beautiful sister.

By the moons, he shouldn't have looked.

"I'm going to dim the lights now. I won't turn them completely off. I know you have pretty good night vision, but I don't, and I might need to use the elimination facilities during the night."

Selon manages to tear his gaze away from the scrap of fabric covering her sex and looks up to her face. She's frowning again but doesn't look afraid. His brain is too muddled to figure out what expression she's wearing, but he knows it's not fear.

"Dim is good," he croaks out.

"Light to ten percent," she calls out, and the shuttle darkens.

He hears her rustle around for a while, situating blankets and getting comfortable. Selon stays perfectly still as he watches her form move.

He can just hear his friends talking over his grave now; *"What happened to poor Selon?"* one would say. *The other would respond, "He died of extreme physical need. There was so much blood in his male member that it burst, and he bled to death. Sad way to go."*

That imaginary conversation almost makes him chuckle and he's able to relax a bit. Lara is quiet now, but not asleep. He starts reviewing documents in his head to distract him as he waits for her to fall asleep so he can slip off to the elimination and cleansing faculties.

"Can I touch you?"

At first, he isn't sure it's Lara talking or his feverish brain making him hear things. He waits, trying to understand what's going on.

"I know you're awake. No one sleeps like that," she tells him, and Selon gives a little groan. He's not sure this is classified as torture by Hissa law, but it should be.

"I don't think touching is a good idea right now." He's proud his voice doesn't sound too hoarse when he speaks. *I can do this*, he thinks. *It's just a matter of control.*

"You want to have sex with me," she states boldly, and Selon jerks into a sitting position. Despite the dim lights, he can easily see her lying on her side, watching him. Now he knows what her expression is—it's interest.

"I won't," he promises.

"I know," she tells him simply. "You've had all kinds of opportunities to accidentally touch me or corner me or make me feel like sleeping with you is an appropriate form of gratitude. But you haven't done any of those things. You never touch me, even when I'm touching you. You're careful to let me get as close as I want to. And you always let me end contact when I want to."

A small, shocked sound comes out of him before he can stop it. She grins. "You didn't think I noticed, did you? I notice everything. I saw you follow me home after the conversation on the tower. You didn't tell anyone. You didn't make me leave until I was ready. Then you show up at Tiran's door the next day and gave me this," she sweeps her hand out to indicate the shuttle. "And now I get to sleep here tonight with the sound of the life support systems humming in the background. I'm deeply grateful to you."

"Is that why you want to touch me?" Selon asks, keeping his voice even despite the emotions and lust raging through his body. "Do you want to thank me that way?"

Lara sits up, letting her hair cover her face, but he can still see her grin get even wider. "If I were going to do something to thank you, I'd fix something at your house."

"Then why are you so interested in touching me?"

"Because I can trust you. I don't get to touch many people. Deena doesn't like to be touched. She puts up with it to make me feel better. Mara lets me hug her, but she starts getting uncomfortable quickly, and I have to let her go. I tried to give Tiran a hug, and he got pale and shaky and ran from the house, and honestly that was probably a good thing because I felt like I was going to throw up." She gives a little shrug. "The idea of trying to touch any other male on this planet freaks me out. I don't think anyone has the level of control that you do."

Selon almost laughs at that. He doesn't have the level of control he wishes he had. "I'm not sure you should trust me right now," he tells her cautiously.

"Because you're horny and have an erection? You've had one off and on all day. But you don't seem to be controlled by it. I know I can trust you to keep your body and instincts in check."

"You saw?" he croaks out, shocked again.

"It's hard to miss," she says wryly. "You're kind of big and it's right there. It almost looks like you're trying to hide a third leg in your pants," Lara chuckles at her joke. He wants to laugh too, but his entire body feels like it's on fire. After her laughter dies down, they both lapse into silence for several minutes.

For the first time, it's Lara who's waiting patiently for him to talk.

"This is probably a bad idea," he finally tells her.

"Maybe," she concedes. Regret flashes across her features, and she ducks her face away from him. "I'm sorry I asked."

Her sudden change from cheerful and heartfelt to sad and resigned rips his heart apart.

"Fine. You can touch me," he tells her, his voice almost harsh. She jumps a little at his sudden words but doesn't look afraid, merely surprised. "I don't think I can do this without a little help," he admits. He looks around and sees an old cord laying on the floor. He leans over to snatch it up and tosses it to Lara. Confused, she grabs it out of the air and looks at it.

"What do you want me to do with this?" she asks as he gets on his knees on the bed and turns his back to her.

"Tie my hands behind my back," he orders her.

She makes a displeased sound. "I don't like that idea."

"It's either this or no touching." He knows his voice is rough, but Lara doesn't flinch. She just gives a little sigh and pulls off her covers and steps across the short distance between bunks.

His bed dips a little as she kneels behind him and ties the cord around his wrists. It bites into his skin when she knots it, but he welcomes the small discomfort.

"Done," she declares and backs away a little. Selon tests the binding and finds it strong enough to hold him. Given time he could probably work himself loose, but for now it will keep him in check.

He lets his head hang for a moment, hoping that whatever happens, he doesn't scare Lara. He takes a deep breath and turns his head to look at her over his shoulder. He doesn't mean to, but his voice sounds like that of a condemned man when he simply says to her, "You may proceed."

CHAPTER 10

Lara watches Selon take several deep breaths as if bracing for torture. When he looks over his shoulder and orders her to proceed, she wonders if she shouldn't call off the whole thing. She doesn't want to make him unhappy, but she wants to explore what he does to her, the things he makes her feel.

As the days have passed, she's felt more and more comfortable with him, able to interact without the threat of a panic attack. He started to feel like Deena to her. A comforting presence that poses no threat.

Well, not quite like Deena. She doesn't feel the urge to touch Deena when she isn't afraid. She doesn't crave Deena's scent like she does Selon. There were numerous times she almost reached out to touch him as they worked side by side.

Absently, she thinks about when she grabbed him to pull him through the hatch and ripped his shirt. The rip at the collar revealed a small strip of pale green skin. She found herself watching that bit of skin on and off during the day, wondering what it would feel like compared to the skin on his hand. Would it be smoother, softer? Or rougher?

Now she has the opportunity to find out what his skin feels like all over his body, but she hesitates. Guilt makes her stomach knot. She reaches forward to untie his hands, ready to tell him she's changed her mind. But before she touches the cord, he shifts himself to face her, and his shirt rides up in the front, revealing a band of his muscled stomach.

All words die in her throat and without conscious thought, she slips her hand under his shirt. His flesh is warm against her palm. The muscles under her hand tighten as she traces along the ridges with fascination. She's vaguely aware he's made a sound but ignores it. She's far too entranced with her current investigation.

She pulls his shirt up higher and uses both hands to explore his chest. He's all tight muscles and power, and yet she doesn't feel intimidated or fearful at all. She leans in a little closer and takes a few deep breaths through her nose. His smell fills her, sending little waves of comfort through her body. "You smell good," she tells him absently. "No one smells as good as you do."

He gives a little grunt, and she looks up at his face. His eyes are shut, and his jaw is clenched so tight that she's surprised she doesn't hear bone cracking. His lips are a hard white line of tension and the scale pattern on his head has turned a deep purple.

"Let me take your shirt off, and you can lie down," she tells him and tugs the shirt off over his head and down his arms to pool around his bound wrists. Selon makes a small choking sound but remains still.

"Did I hurt you?" she asks anxiously, but he shakes his head quickly. She pushes on his chest gently, urging him to lie back on the bed. "Lie down so you can stretch out your legs. It can't be good to kneel on them like that for long."

With a total lack of grace that almost makes Lara giggle, Selon falls sideways, stretching his leg out. She can see the outline of his erection running down one leg of his pants and bites her lip. Now she wonders what that part of his anatomy feels like.

"Should I take your pants off too?" she asks, hoping he'll say yes. "So you can be more comfortable?"

"Not a good idea," Selon grits out between clenched teeth. Lara doesn't move and stares intensely at his mouth, thinking. Finally, Selon opens his eyes and looks at her.

"I've never kissed anyone," she confesses and watches his eyes go wide with surprise. "I've seen Deena do it, and Tiran and Mara do it all the time."

"Never? Not even," Selon starts to say, then stops with a look of consternation. "I'm sorry. I didn't mean to bring that up."

"No, it's' fine," Lara assures him with a small smile. "I've never kissed or been kissed, even when I was held by the raiders. The captain and crew were all Diniki. Kissing isn't part of their makeup. I'd like to know what it's like."

A mildly panicked expression crosses Selon's face. "Maybe you should tie my legs down also."

Lara frowns. "I don't like that your hands are tied. I'm not tying anything else of yours down. Now, may I please kiss you?"

"Moons preserve me," Selon mutters and then nods. "If I scare you, please drug me," he begs. "This shuttle has a box of drug guns full of sedatives. Grab one and inject me if you feel threatened at all."

Lara almost laughs at his desperate demands. "I promise to drug you if I feel fear."

"You need to mean it, Lara. You need to know that if I cause you fear, it will rip my heart in two," Selon tells her earnestly. "I'd rather die than make you afraid of me."

Comprehension dawns and Lara finally understands all his reluctance. Her earlier humor disappears. He knows her. He's watched her struggle. Seen her at her most vulnerable. He's doesn't want to be the reason she trembles from dread. He doesn't want to be the reason for a panic attack.

For the first time in her life, she needs to reassure someone else. She's the one in power right now. The one that has the power to give comfort.

It makes her bold.

"Don't be afraid," she murmurs. "I trust you. More than I trust the sister I barely know any more. I trust you as much as I trust Deena. You're a good and honorable male, Selon. You'd never do anything to make me afraid."

With those words, his face softens, the strain easing a little. "I would never intentionally hurt you."

"I don't think you could accidentally hurt me either," she says. "Even now, when you fear you might lose control you make me tie your hands. That's not something the men outside would do. No other Hissa would even think to offer, let alone demand it." He grumbles something under his breath at her words. All she catches is "…death of me." Poor Selon. She's testing his resolve.

Hopefully, this whole experiment will end well for both of them.

"Tell me what you feel around me," she asks, teasing her fingers along the line of muscled flesh above his pants.

"Your aroma is so tantalizing, and I can even taste you on

my tongue when we are close. It's like a drug and—" He stops and swallows hard. "I think perhaps all of you is addicting," he finishes. His words make her heartbeat increase, and her skin feels hot.

"Do you know you smell good too?" Lara asks, wanting to draw his attention away from his concern of causing her fear.

"I thought humans didn't have much of a sense of smell," he says.

"Natural born might not, but I'm Decanted. I love your smell. When I hold your hand and wrap myself around your arm, your scent fills my nose. It makes me feel good. It makes my brain calm." She scoots a little closer until her chest is touching his shoulder. The contact makes him jerk a little, but she doesn't stop until her mouth is close to his. He looks hungry and scared at the same time.

She understands those two conflicting emotions. How often has she wanted the comforting touch of another but was too scared of repercussions to act on her impulse? She and Selon might have more in common than she realized. Both of them are fearful of the emotional minefield that is her traumatized brain.

"I want to know if touching you has the same effect as your smell." She closes her eyes and brushes her lips across his, loving the feel. She pulls away, her lips tingling a little from the contact.

He closes his eyes and parts his lips slightly, inviting her to deepen the kiss. Just like when they talk, she's in charge of how far this will go. That makes her feel bold enough to try what she's seen Tiran and Mara do so many times. Acting before she can consider it, she closes her mouth over his.

His taste explodes across her tongue and suddenly her body feels tight and needy. She eagerly runs her tongue over his sharp canines and feels him shudder. He tentatively touches his tongue to hers, and she gives a little moan.

She draws back a bit, shaking with something she can't describe. "You taste so good," she whispers.

"You do too," he tells her. "Do you like kissing? It doesn't make you feel . . ." He stops, trying to find the right words. She can guess what he's thinking.

"None of this brings back bad memories. None of this is like anything I've ever experienced," she assures him. "I'd like to kiss you again."

For the first time since she asked to touch him, he smiles. Some of the worry disappears from his face. "I'd like that too."

She strains forward, locking her lips to his, letting his smell fill her lungs and his taste fill her mouth. She moves too abruptly, and one of his canines pushes against her lip. It doesn't hurt. It feels oddly erotic, making her very aware of the throbbing clit and moisture gathering between her legs.

She's never paid much attention to that area of her sex before. She washes it, cares for it, and curses it when she bleeds every month. But other than that, she doesn't think about it much. It's something she just has. Something others want to abuse. Until now, she never considered it a source of pleasure.

Now she has an uncontrollable urge to rub herself against Selon. Rub her needy sex against him. Covering him with her feminine juices seems like an added bonus. A way to claim territory. A way to mark him as belonging to her.

Abruptly, she pulls away and hears him give a low sound of distress. She doesn't say anything, just sits up to pull off the small, tight top covering her breasts. Then she flops back down and pushes her hips up to tug off her panties. Naked, she pushes herself back against Selon's side, thinking to find a way to alleviate the need in her, but not sure how.

"Lara, what are you doing?" Selon asks, his voice a little shaky. She looks up at his face, feeling bewildered.

"I'm not sure. I feel things, down here," she points to between her legs. "And I want it to feel even better, but I'm not sure how."

Selon's mouth gapes open. "You've never had a climax?"

"Do you mean sex? I've had that. I'm not a virgin," she says with a shake of her head, frustrated. "This isn't like that. This feels good." Selon closes his eyes, and the scale pattern on his head flashes from purple, the color of passion, to brown, the color of growing irritation. And Lara wonders how she managed to upset him.

"You were raped. That's not sex," he tells her bluntly.

"It's not?" This is news to her. She'd just always assumed that's what sex was, and all the women she knew put up with it because they were forced, or because they love the males in their lives. Well, except Deena, who doesn't have a choice because of her biology.

"Sex is when both parties enjoy what's happening," Selon explains, and Lara feels a little hitch in her heart. If she's never had sex before maybe she could try it for the first time with Selon.

"Are we having sex right now?" she asks, very unsure of her knowledge base.

"We are close to it. What we're doing right now is seduction, touching with hands and mouth to make each partner feel pleasure and heighten awareness of each other." He sounds clinical suddenly, and Lara withdraws slightly.

She sits up and looks to see if he still has an erection. She reaches down and rests her hand over his hard cock, feeling its outline through the pants. It's still hard but perhaps not as much as before. Selon gives a small groan as she touches him, and she feels it get harder under her touch. The scales on his head flush purple again.

"If we had sex, would you need to put this inside of me?" she asks.

"Only if you wanted. There are many things we can do that don't involve penetration," Selon tells her, his voice not entirely steady.

"What else can we do?" She thinks he'll say rubbing, but instead he rolls on his side and nuzzles her shoulder with his face.

"I want to put my mouth on you," he confesses.

"You want to lick me?" She's interested but confused.

"Lick and suck and other things," he tells her. "Bring one of your breasts to my mouth. Let me show you."

Excited to feel more new things, she lowers her chest as Selon rolls over on his back. When she's close enough, he opens his mouth and closes it around her nipple. She gives a strangled gasp and clutches at his chest. He sucks gently, and she moans at the sensations rioting through her body. As he tugs with his lips, the throbbing between her legs intensifies. She reaches down to touch that part of herself and feels a wave of intense pleasure go through her when she runs her fingers over a nub of flesh just in front of her vagina. It's never felt so good to touch herself before.

Selon pulls his mouth away from her breast and follows the line of her arm to the hand between her thighs. "I can put my mouth there too."

She doesn't even hesitate. She swings her legs over him and crawls forward until her sex hovers over his face. Then she stops cold.

"I could smother you," she worries and starts to dismount, but Selon makes a sound of intense discomfort.

"No, please," he begs. "I can smell you! I want to taste you so bad. Please, let me put my mouth on you. You can't hurt me! Please." Shaken and unsure, she pulls herself off him, despite the sound of pain he makes.

"Roll onto your side," she urges and lays herself back

down, putting the Y of her legs right at his face. She parts her legs, and Selon doesn't need any further urging. He moves his head forward, using her thigh as a pillow and nudging her left leg out of the way. She pulls it up towards her chest, and he buries his face into her folds.

She thinks she should tell him to be careful with his teeth, but then he's sucking that little nub of flesh into his mouth. Sensations crash through her, and she can't breathe.

She arches back and moans as his mouth works. She can't stop her hips from undulating against his face and hopes he can breathe despite her movements. She wishes he could touch her breasts while his mouth is on her and curses him for making her tie his hands.

She feels a strange kind of tension building in her. She's not sure what it means, but what he's doing with his lips and tongue seems to make it worse. Her entire body feels too hot, and her skin feels too tight. She wants to make him stop and increase the pressure at the same time.

He grazes her with one of his canines, and Lara screams, her first climax making every muscle in her body flex. All the air is forced out of her lungs, and she gasps for air as the pleasure crashes over her.

Selon is moving his tongue in slow, deliberate strokes now, instead of the earlier frenzied pace. The movement causes her entire body to quiver. Finally, she can't take it anymore and pulls herself away from him and rolls on her back, letting the air cool her overheated skin.

He scoots forward and rests his head on her stomach. Absently, she reaches down and starts stroking her hand over the now purplish-blue scale pattern.

"I've never felt that before," she admits when she can finally talk.

"Did you like it?"

She grins down at him. "I did. Now I know what all the fuss is about and why Tiran and Mara are so noisy every night."

Selon chuckles and then shifts uncomfortably. Lara remembers his hands are still tied and sits up to untie him. He moves his head out of her lap to allow her access. As she leans over, his erection presses against her leg and he gives a small groan.

"You said sex is when both parties enjoy it," she says as she unties his hands.

"Yes," he answers cautiously. He doesn't protest as she

unties him, only brings his hands in front of him and gives a little sigh of relief. He must have more confidence in his control now.

"But I don't think you got to feel what I did." She wants to give him the same pleasure he gave her, so she reaches for his pants. He stops her by putting his hands over hers and sitting up.

"That's not necessary," he tells her. "It's intensely satisfying to watch you climax."

"Is there any way we can do that at the same time?" she asks, bringing her face close enough to kiss him again. He tastes a little like her, and she decides it's not bad. What would he taste like if she put her mouth on his erection? The thought intrigues her. "I'd like to give you pleasure too. Maybe feel you in my mouth?"

"I'm not sure that's a good idea," he starts, then gives a little moan. "You tempt me too much."

"Show me how we can enjoy it together. This is new to me. Show me what sex is like, I want to experience more of it."

Selon tenses. "I'm not sure I'm going to survive this."

CHAPTER

11

"Would you take off your pants now?"

Lara's question makes Selon freeze for a moment, caught between the desire to strip and the almost equally intense need to flee the shuttle.

"My male part is engorged," he warns her.

"I'm very aware of that fact," she says with a light laugh. "I could feel it when I leaned against you, and I can see the outline. I'm not scared."

Selon decides to be honest. "I don't know how you've been abused in the past, and I don't want to trigger any bad memories or panic attacks."

Her smile disappears, replaced by a thoughtful expression. "Nothing we've done so far is anything like what they did to me. You don't grab me or hold me. You don't put your weight against me to pin me in place against a wall."

"I do want to touch you," he tells her and holds his breath for the answer.

She looks eager. "More of what you did with your mouth? Because I liked that. A lot!"

Her enthusiasm makes him smile. "Yes, more of that. But I'd like to put my hands on your body too."

"I want to put my hands on your body also. That's why you need to take off your pants." As she talks, her body jumps up and down a little, as if she's too excited to remain still.

"You're very focused," he comments with a little shake of his head.

She shrugs. "I can only do one thing at a time because that one thing takes up all my attention. Right now, the one thing I want is to do more of this stuff with you."

He can't fault that. It's all he wants to do as well. "I'll go slow with the touching. Just tell me no if you need me to stop. I might make some noises. But that can't be helped."

"Right. Beware of noises, tell you if I don't like something, and we go slow," she agrees and crawls a little closer to him.

If he thought the smell of her during the day was bad, he wasn't at all prepared for the elixir of desire that she is now. With his mouth full of her sex, her taste on his tongue, and her scent filling his lungs, he is in a strange place of wonder and pain. Now, his hands shake from need.

In an attempt to calm himself down a little before he gives into impulse and snatches her to himself, he closes his eyes. Then he feels a tug at his pants and looks down to find her trying to work the clasp open. Waiting any longer is not an option.

"This is stubborn," she mutters, and he brushes her fingers aside and runs his finger over the closure. It opens at his touch, and he feels a slight bit of relief as his engorged shaft springs free. Then she's there, trying to pull them down. The way he is sitting makes it impossible and he's not sure he can stand at the moment, so he lies down and lifts his hips the same way she did earlier. She pulls them down past his knees, then he kicks them off.

He hears her give a little gasp and looks to see her wide eyes locked on his male member. There's no fear in her face, just surprise and curiosity. "Can I touch it?" she asks already reaching for him. "Diniki don't look anything like you."

He doesn't get a chance to respond before her hand is closing around his shaft. It's all he can do not thrust his hips up and push himself deeper into her grip. He's been so controlled for so long that her touch shatters him. A low growl vibrates out of him, and her hand freezes as his eyes flutter shut. By the moons, her touch is like nothing he's ever experienced before.

"You don't like that?" He opens his eyes to see her peering down at him anxiously. "Is my hand too rough? Should I put my mouth there instead? Like you did for me."

He wants to tell her anything she does to him is amazing but once again, she's turned his brain to mush. His eloquent brain, so good at talking to others, so good at communicating thoughts and emotions, has completely forgotten any language he's ever learned.

Does he even know his name right now?

"Selon? Should I stroke you with my hand or use my mouth?" she asks again. "Your mouth felt good. Maybe you would like my mouth on you."

He nods his head and in his fevered brain that movement is meant to say, 'your hand feels wonderful, please don't stop.'

"Oh good, I like that better," she says, and he's confused because she takes her hand away. No, didn't he just agree that she should keep touching him?

He thinks to reach out and draw her hand back when her mouth is on him, warm and wet. He bows off the bed, unprepared for so much sensation. Her hands now free, she touches his chest with one hand, running her fingers over his muscles and dancing along his skin. Her other hand dips lower, exploring the soft flesh under his male member, finding his sensitive seed sack and tugging gently on it.

He would scream with pleasure if there was any air in his lungs. His climax is imminent. He should warn her. He needs to speak words so he can tell her to pull away from him. Then it's too late and he's roaring as pleasure floods his system. She makes a little noise of surprise as he empties into her mouth, but she doesn't stop.

It isn't until he gently tugs at a lock of her hair that she releases him from her mouth. He pops free and she sits back, looking at him with interest and excitement. Her lips are swollen, cheeks flushed, and pupils dilated. She enjoyed what she was doing, and it fills him with relief, allowing him to truly relish the languid aftereffects of his orgasm.

"Was that good? You could give me instructions. I don't mind," she tells him earnestly. "Nothing I've known is like this. I've never been with a male like you before. I want to make you feel as good as you made me feel."

"You're perfect," he manages to gasp out, drawing her down to lie next to him. He starts to put an arm over her, wanting to cuddle, but she tenses so instead he pulls her arm over him, letting her be in charge of the embrace. She gives a soft laugh and scoots closer, throwing a leg over him and resting her arm across his chest.

"You're not like the Diniki at all," she tells him, her voice soft and body relaxed.

"No?"

"Where you're smooth and thick they are thin and have hard ridges. And there are two," she gestures vaguely to his softening male member. "Two mating limbs. Their females lay eggs and have two separate places for males to enter to fertilize eggs."

Selon had to fight to keep from tensing up. "You don't have two vaginas," he states simply.

She goes silent but doesn't get tense. It's almost like he can hear her thinking. Debating how much to share. When she does speak, what she says surprises him.

"I'm afraid to tell you. I'm afraid you won't want to touch me anymore."

He already has a good idea about what happened but wants her to confide in him. "I'm sure there is nothing you could say that would do that. If you wish to talk, I want to listen. If you're not ready, I can wait. You're in control here, sweet Lara, no one else but you."

Those were the exact right words to say because he feels her give a decisive nod against his chest.

"Diniki breed standing up," she explains, her tone clinical. "The males have these grabbing appendages on their waist to hold a female still and then they pierce them with their two male parts." Her tone is lacking in any emotion, almost as if she's giving a lecture at a university.

"I've seen a picture of a male Diniki," Selon says neutrally. "They are tall, like a Hissa, but much thinner and look a little reptilian."

"With rough skin," she elaborates, then falls silent for a while. She takes a deep breath and continues. "They pulled me out of the escape pod and tore off my clothes to see if I was biologically compatible. They had a hallway where they chained people up so the crew could use them as they liked. If the species wasn't sexually compatible, they would poke a hole or two in them and fill it with sealant, so the slave didn't bleed out. I watched a Timmieran being raped while they examined me. He had two wounds in his back they used. The sealant might have kept him from bleeding out, but it didn't stop the pain."

Selon doesn't hear any tears in her voice, no pain. She's detached from the memory.

"They were delighted to find I was sexually compatible with two holes, they called one my breeding hole and the other my elimination hole. They were just about to chain me up to the wall when the captain showed up. He decided I would be his private slave and put a collar on me and dragged me to his room."

"It wasn't horrible," she tells him flatly, and Selon just barely keeps himself from roaring in rage at the casual statement. "He pinned me against a wall and used his grabbers to hold me in position. It hurt when he put himself in me but triggering the obedience collar would've hurt more. Being given to the crew would have been horrendous, so I guess that means I was lucky. It wasn't as bad as it could've been."

Never letting that happen to her in the first place would have been better, he thinks, wishing with every cell in his body he could've been there to prevent such abuse.

"He decided he'd keep me. Told me if I left the room, I better hide because if the crew caught me, they would use me too. My only duty was to be in his room at a certain time every day." She takes another deep breath, steadying herself. "That's why I hid in the engine room. Diniki have very sensitive hearing and none of them liked going back there. If I just stayed in the captain's cabin, they would've cornered me while he wasn't there. The sound of the engine mostly kept them away."

"It was your safe place," Selon comments.

"Yes. It was also a place to do something. To not have to think about the captain or the crew. I could fuss with the engine and concentrate on something in my hands instead of my fear. After a while, they realized I was good with that stuff and gave me clothes and privileges. But I still had to be careful. I got caught once. It was only two of them, but it hurt to have one right after another use me and then I had to get back to the cabin to service the captain. I learned quickly how to find ways to get around the ship in secret. Paths that kept me hidden or were too small for them to fit. I learned to hide and be quiet. I learned to only half sleep and grab meals when no one was around."

Selon wants to hug her but knows it's a bad idea. "Would you do me a favor?"

She tenses and starts to draw away from him. "I'm sorry. I knew I shouldn't have told. Now you don't want me touching you anymore."

Selon grabs a hand and tugs it back over his chest. "Just the opposite. I'd like you to touch me more please," he begs. "You hung on me like a backpack earlier. Would you do something similar to my front?"

She sits up and looks at his chest, then throws a leg over and straddles him. She settles her body down until her upper body rests on his and her knees rest on either side of his hips. She rests her head on him and gives a small, contented sigh.

"I'm sure everyone thinks the worst part is what the Diniki did to me," she continues, running her hand up and down his chest as she talks, almost like she's petting him. "But it wasn't. The worst was what they did to the people they captured and chained in the hallway. They all died. Some lasted a few months. Some only lasted a day or two. But they all died eventually. And that hallway was almost always busy. I'd try and sneak in there sometimes, to give them food and water or comfort. But it was risky because the hallway had a lot of foot traffic, so I couldn't do it often."

"You were just as much a victim as those people," he tells her gently, understanding now that she's also suffering from survivor's guilt.

"But I could have done more," she insists, and for the first time in this conversation, he hears emotion in her voice. "They begged me to kill them. Every time I tried to help; they would all beg me to end their suffering. I could have. I had access to tools. I could have killed them all." She takes a shaky breath. "But I couldn't do it. I couldn't kill any of them, no matter how much they begged. I'm a coward."

She starts silently crying, tears falling on Selon's chest. He raises his hands and carefully places one on her hand and the other on her hair, hoping these are two neutral spots that won't trigger her fear.

She wiggles her hand out from under his and he pulls away, thinking it was too much contact. But then she snatches his hand and drags it between their bodies, very much like she'd done before.

"You're not a coward," he tells her. "You survived. You survived in a place no one else could have, and it's not just because the captain singled you out. You survived because you're smart and clever. You couldn't kill those people because you value life so much. As long as they were alive, there was a chance. You couldn't give up on that chance. You weren't a coward, you were hopeful." She sobs quietly as he talks.

She hiccups and tightens her knees against his hips, giving him a kind of hug. "Please keep talking," she requests. "Your voice makes my heart hurt less."

"You're safe now, but the fear is still there. You spent so

many years living in fear, existing on the edge of survival that you don't know how to turn that part of yourself off. Some medications can help, but more than anything, it's going to take time."

"I'm broken," she tells him, and another small sob comes out of her.

"No, never," he assures her and kisses her gently on her forehead. "What's the most common thing to break on these shuttles?"

Caught by surprise, she answers without thought. "Planetary range finder. It's powered by engine voltage instead of going through an exchanger like the life support systems, so they're always burning out."

"Would you throw away a whole shuttle if just the planetary range finder broke?"

She gives a watery chuckle. "Am I the shuttle in this question?"

"Perhaps. I just wanted to make my point. We fix things. We heal things. We don't just throw them away. Especially things as beautiful, smart, and wonderful as you."

"You might change your mind the more time you spend with me," she warns him with a sniff, but she's not crying any more.

"I'd love to see if you could," Selon challenges her. "But I warn you, you'll need to spend years trying to convince me you're not worthy. And I'll spend those years refusing to believe you."

She goes still against him, and he lets her breathe and think. "Would you be willing to be with me for years?" she asks. "Talk to me? Touch me?"

The rest of our lives, he thinks. *I could do this for the rest of our lives.*

"As long as you need me," he promises her instead.

She snuggles against him, wiggling her hips a little to get more comfortable. "That's good. I like that."

They talk more, but not about her captivity with the Diniki raiders. Mostly, she tells him all about the many things she had to do to keep Ally running. He winces when he hears about some of the more dangerous tasks she performed in space, normally done safely when a ship is docked at a secure location with atmosphere. He feels her joy when she tells him about the fun times she and Deena shared and the occasional funny mishap or adventure.

"How did you and Deena meet?" he asks. The information on her escape from the raiders is scanty and doesn't include the months following her release. Before she and Deena started working independently. When anyone asked Deena, she gives a sarcastic response and brushes them off.

"Deena was on the crew that saved me," Lara explains easily.

"I read the raiders were captured by a civilian patrol," he mentions.

"There are some areas where there aren't any military or law-keeping ships. The planets in those systems set up bounties. If you capture a raider ship, you could turn it in for the bounty. The Revenge was one of them, and Deena was their pilot." Lara gives a little shudder. "She was the only human and the only female on board. I don't know how she did it. That crew was almost twenty strong and she had to share a berth with two others. They slept in shifts, so they were never actually in the bunk together. But still, she didn't have any privacy or a safe place to be alone."

"Do you think it bothered her?"

"No, she's very different than I am. She's not scared of anything," Lara tells him confidently.

"She's scared," he tells her. The daily reports he reads about her conduct among the Hissa paint a vivid picture of someone hiding their fears and weakness with bravado. "She just isn't scared of the same things you're scared of." Lara gives a small sound of disagreement but doesn't continue that line of conversation.

"Anyway, when they captured the ship, I was hiding, scared that whoever had us now was going to be even worse than the Diniki. I didn't know it, but after they imprisoned the Diniki on their ship, they were going to expose the inside of the raider ship to the vacuum of space to sterilize it. I would've died. But Deena noticed some of my clothes in the captain's quarters while she was doing a sweep. She went searching for me, even stood up to her captain to delay departure so she could look for me."

"I'm surprised they listened to her," Selon comments. Bounty hunters aren't known for their patience and more often than not they bring home dead bounty instead of living. The pay is the same either way.

"She's the best pilot they could get," Lara explains. "One of the reasons the Revenge was so successful was because Deena is so skilled. One of the crew said she seemed to be able to bend spacecraft to her will."

"So, she found you?" Selon urges her to continue her story.

"I was hiding above the corridor where they used to keep the prisoners chained. There weren't any prisoners there when the

Revenge captured the ship, the last one had died the day before. That's the first time I saw her. She was calling out in Space Standard that I was safe, and she would make sure I was taken care of. I was scared to trust her but figured she was human and female, so she was my best chance. I dropped down in front of her." Lara chuckles at the memory. "She almost shot me."

"Moons preserve me," Selon gets out, his whole body jerking in shock at her words. She pulls an arm out from between them and pets the top of his head, comforting him. This woman is too wonderful for words.

"I stood there, in front of her in the corridor, shaking and crying. I couldn't seem to talk, but she just knew," Lara tells him. "She got me on the Revenge, kept the men away from me, and found me a little maintenance corridor right off the steering thrusters control shaft to bed down in. It was hot and loud and perfect."

"What happened after that?"

"The place they went to turn in the raiders for money was several weeks journey and I got bored. I started playing with the engine. No one noticed until I had to take life support down for a little while. The captain was furious. He thought I was trying to sabotage the ship. He sent men to drag me onto the bridge. I had a panic attack and fought them, but they easily subdued me." Selon brings her hand down from where she's petting his head and kisses her palm.

"It felt horrible to be so trapped after having days of freedom and no worries. I thought that was it, I was going to be chained up in a corridor and wait for death. But Deena was there and talked for me. I couldn't talk, all I could do was cry. She told them what I was doing, but the captain still didn't trust me. He put an obedience collar on me, keyed it to his voice, and told me if I didn't get the life support up within the hour, he'd call out Obedience 3 over the ship coms."

"That would've killed you!" Despite his best intentions, his voice is too loud and full of outrage. He can't imagine how much fear Lara must have felt. Already suffering from panic attacks, then shackled by male crew members and brought before an irate captain. Then threatened with death for doing the kind of repairs that came so naturally to her.

"I was more scared for Deena," Lara admits. "I didn't mind dying at that point. I thought it would be pleasant to be dead and no longer feel fear and panic. But Deena's life was on the line now too. The captain threatened to flush her out an airlock because she was the one who gave me access to the engine."

"He wouldn't have," Selon tells her with confidence. "She was too valuable as a pilot." He didn't comment about Lara's willingness to die. Anyone suffering that way couldn't be faulted for feeling like death might be a blessing.

"I know that now," she tells him. "I came to understand that later, but at the time, I thought I was fighting for her life. It took everything in me to keep the panic in check and finish the repairs so the life support could come back on. Not only did I get that running again, but the engines ran better too because I was able to clean out the transition fuel beds. The captain was pleased and took the collar off. Even though he was friendly after that, I hid in the engine compartment for the rest of the flight. When we finally reached Gililos to turn over the bounty, Deena took her share and left the ship with me, quitting her job. She got us a job together, and we worked until we earned enough to buy Ally."

"I have a feeling there's a lot more to that than those few pithy sentences," he says with a small shake of his head.

"Good times, I promise," she tells him quickly. "Deena looked after me. She kept me safe. I owe her everything. And now she's stuck on this planet because of me, and they won't let her fly."

"I'll talk to the Council," Selon promises. He now realizes Lara isn't just having issues with her own experiences but also suffering from deep guilt for causing Deena unhappiness. "I'm sure I can work something out so Deena can fly again."

"You seem to have a lot of influence," Lara comments thoughtfully.

"At the moment I do," Selon agrees and wonders when he should tell her he was assigned to her. He's worried about frightening her, worried she'll see it as a betrayal. And more worried than he wants to admit that he'll never get to touch her again.

He thinks about the communications he gets from the Council requesting updates on Lara's condition and demands for her to start meeting new men. He keeps putting them off. Because of his reputation, they trust him, so far. That could all change if they find out how intimate he and Lara have become.

There is no way this can end well for me; he thinks with resignation. All he can hope for is that by the time the Council realizes what's going on between him and Lara, she'll be strong enough to function well without him.

CHAPTER

12

"I want to know what it feels like to have you inside me."
Of all the things Selon expected to hear first thing in the morning, that was not one of them. He goes from being partially awake and content to lie there and enjoy the feel of Lara, to fully awake and tense.

Lara is back on top of him, staring down at him expectantly. They fell asleep in this position but shifted through the night. They must have finally ended up in their original bodily arrangement. And now Lara is awake and staring at him as if she's thinking about what she wants from him.

It's good that Hissa can function on very little sleep because he spent most of the night awake and watching Lara. He was much too fearful to sleep, worried that while he slept, he might roll himself into a position that would cause her distress.

His diligence is rewarded because she looks rested and eager. She props up on her arms, staring down at him with an intensity he's only seen her use when examining engine parts.

"What time is it?" he asks, wishing his brain is more awake.

"I don't know," she bounces on him a little, making him wheeze out a breath. "I want to do more of what we did last night." He feels his cock harden and thinks wryly, *I might not be awake, but he certainly is.*

"We should check in with Tiran and Mara," he gets out, grabbing her shoulders and tugging her down to lie flat on top of him. It doesn't help. She just seems to be vibrating with energy. Then he realizes that he grabbed her, and she didn't react badly. It fills him with joy to know she has so little fear of him now.

"We can check in later. I want to have more sex now."

He lets her pull away from him to sit back up. Her sex is sitting on his hardening cock and her wiggling is quickly driving him insane. "You did warn me you focus completely on whatever task is at hand," he says with a small grin.

"I can feel you getting ready again." She grins back, staring down at where their bodies meet. She wiggles again and gives a little sound of pleasure when his erection rubs on her clit. She's wet and her juices are already coating him.

"Let me use my mouth on you again." He urges her hips toward his head, but she pushes back against him.

"I like it here," she pouts and grabs his hands to put them on her breasts. "And I like that." He obliges her by palming both breasts, enjoying the soft feel of them under his fingers.

"Let me pleasure you with my mouth, then you can see if you want to try penetration," he tries to bargain, and she opens her eyes to glare at him.

She rubs herself against him a little more vigorously, and he moans. If she keeps that up there won't be an issue: he'll come before the argument is over. "Please be still, *shamira*," he begs.

"*Shamira?*"

"It's a flower here on Hissa. It's considered to be the most beautiful and it only blooms once every decade. We have a festival in honor of it. You make me think of it. The flowers are delicate and easily damaged, but the plant is hardy and a good survivor."

She stops rubbing. "I like that name."

"It fits you, sweet *shamira*. You smell even better than that fragrant flower," he growls out. "Now put yourself in my mouth before I start crying."

"You wouldn't!" she giggles, but obligingly moves off him to lie next to him. Her face turns serious as he gets on his knees and moves down to crouch between her legs. "Will I enjoy you inside me, even if we do this first?"

"This will make sure you enjoy the second part even more," he promises and dives between her legs before she can ask him any more questions. She gasps, and he feels her thighs tighten around his head. He adjusts them both so her heels rest on his back, putting his shoulders between her legs so she can't clamp down on him again.

"That feels so good," she whispers and then gives a little gasp again. He brings his hand up to her body, drawing his finger along her labia, testing the entrance to her vagina. She moves against him and doesn't protest. He pushes one finger in, she feels slick and warm, and his movements only make her push against him more.

Careful to keep from accidentally puncturing her with his canines while he sucks and licks her clit, he slowly pulls his finger out, and she undulates under him with a little cry of pleasure and surprise.

He works a second finger into her, and the response is immediate and intense. She bows off the bed, giving a small scream, and her juices flow over his finger. She pants and finally pushes at his head and shoulders to get him to withdraw his mouth from her sensitive flesh.

Once he's no longer stroking her with his tongue, she collapses back, breathing hard. Selon raises his head up to see her face, and his heart almost bursts with happiness when he sees her grinning up at him with half closed lids.

"I like this," she tells him.

"I guessed that," he responds and moves to lie down next to her, but she grasps his hips with her legs, trapping him.

"You haven't had your pleasure yet," she pushes herself up on her elbows, looking down at his hard cock with greedy eyes.

"I don't need to," he starts, and she rolls her eyes at him.

"Don't start that again," she huffs out, then wiggles her hips against him. "How do you fit inside me? Can we do it facing each other, or do I need to turn around?" She frowns and shakes her head. "I don't want to turn around. You'll have to figure out how to do it this way."

He knows she's thinking of the Diniki and is quick to reassure her. "There are a lot of ways. Let's try it sitting."

She gives him a questioning look but doesn't look alarmed. He grabs her waist and hauls her up until she's on his lap, her legs around his lower back. The tip of his shaft sits against her, and he moves her a little until he pierces her slightly.

"Tell me to stop. At any point tell me to stop," he orders her. Her eyes have closed again, concentrating on what she's feeling. She opens her eyes and puts her forehead to his.

"Do. Not. Stop," she orders, making him grin. He slides her forward and down, letting his erection slide into her, slow and steady. Her eyes go wide, and her mouth forms a small O, then her head drops to his shoulder. "More," she moans as her body quivers.

He pulls her against him and when her sensitive clit rubs against the base of him, she gives a small cry of pleasure and starts moving against him with strong jerking movements, lost in the sensations.

He tries to remain still, letting her work herself back and forth on his shaft, letting her find the spot she wants to rub. A film of sweat is soon coating both of them, and Selon isn't sure he can hold himself back much longer.

When her climax tightens her muscles, milking his cock inside her, he can't help but find his pleasure, growling as he fills her with his seed. "You're so beautiful," he groans out. "My sweet *shamira*. My wonderful, rare *shamira*."

Panting, he rises on his knees and shifts them both so when he lies down, she's on top of him. They lay there, sweat drying on their skin, both trying to gain their breath while little fissures of pleasure seem to make them twitch.

He's just about to fall back to sleep when Lara rears up and slaps both her hands down on his chest. "Get up, get up!" she orders cheerfully. "There are repairs to do!"

Before he can even growl at her, she's off of him and skipping to the small cleansing unit in the shuttle.

She's going to kill me; he thinks and slumps back down on the bed after watching her lovely ass disappear into the small room. *One way or another, she's going to be the death of me.*

CHAPTER "13"

Lara is covered in engine lubricant. Her black hair, secured in a small ponytail at the back of her head, is starting to come loose again, getting in her way. And she just banged her head for the third time on the same elbow joint. "Stupid engineers," she hisses and feels Selon put a hand on her leg, the only part of her not buried in the booster engine that's finally mounted on the shuttle.

Even though Selon's repeatedly told her that there's no set timeline to get the cargo shuttle done, she pushes herself hard. If she can get it done quickly and efficiently, and it works well, then hopefully that will be enough for the Council to allow her to continue this work on other shuttles. At the start, she mentally set a goal for herself and is running half a day behind now. Mild frustration is making her clumsy, and the pain she feels from the clumsiness is feeding the frustration.

"Are you well? Maybe we should take a break? Do you need food?" his concerned voice echoes around her inside the gas pressurization chamber.

She wants to snap at him to stop asking her those same questions every time she makes a sound, but she knows he just wants to be helpful. In an attempt to make up for the time she lost this morning, she worked steadily all day, barely stopping to eat. She can feel fatigue pulling at her.

"Lara?"

She wants to ignore him, brush off his unease, but instead she wiggles out of the compartment. "Coming out," she calls to him, then lets him take her by the arm to help her jump down. He frowns when he sees her face, "You should rest. This is enough for today."

Stifling the urge to argue, Lara gives in and acknowledges her weariness. She knows better than to work while tired, so she leans over to set the tool down. "You're right. I just really wanted to do a test start on the boosters by the end of today."

"Tomorrow, sweet *shamira*," Selon promises and places a chaste kiss on her forehead. "There's no need to rush. This is a test shuttle only. I promise everyone will wait patiently for your results."

Lara eyes the shuttle. "If we get here a little earlier tomorrow, we might finish by the early evening."

"You could ask me to do more," he grumbles under his breath. "I'm strong and not useless."

She looks over at him, surprised to see embarrassment on his face. "I do ask you to help."

"Not often. I know I don't know the names of all the tools, but you don't need to climb out of the engine to grab something and then all the way back in. If you describe it, I could hand it to you. I can lift things. I'm strong." She's never heard him sound so insecure or frustrated. It's adorable.

"I'm sorry," she tells him sincerely. "It doesn't occur to me to ask for help. I've never really had help before. It's always just been me."

Selon looks a little shame-faced. "I should have known that. I'm sorry for saying anything. You work so hard, and I just want to be helpful."

"I'll ask you for more help from now on," she promises. Now that she's no longer distracted by work, she realizes she's starving. "Can we get food now?"

"I've been told many sent gifts of food when they heard about you being forced to spend the night in the repair bay. It was all taken to Tiran and Mara, so there should be plenty waiting for us when we arrive. Everyone was disbanded from the port late last night, and not only are there two guards waiting to escort us, but the military set up a perimeter around the port to keep large numbers from gathering again."

She gives a little nod and follows him to the front of the repair bay. She hesitates at the door, fearful despite his reassurance. He steps out, then stops and looks back at her. Because he knows she's a little worried, he wants to give her all the time she needs to prepare herself. He always gives her time and space. Always lets her decide the pace.

Rewarding him with a big smile, she steps out in the fading light. Woken and another guard she doesn't know flank them, and she looks at them both nervously, quickly catching Selon's hand to hold in hers as they walk.

Woken eyes their joined hands but doesn't say anything.

"Would you like to take a private transport or walk?" Selon asks her. "The trams are out of the question at this time of day. They'll be far too crowded."

Lara isn't paying attention to him. Her whole focus is on the guard she doesn't know. Her mind fills with all the things they've talked about as she worked on the shuttle. All the things he's told her.

It's time to stop being afraid, she tells herself. *It's time to let go of the past. I'm in control here.*

Right now feels like it's time to put that belief into practice. Still holding onto Selon's hand, she takes a small step toward the guard she doesn't know and lets her eyes meet his. She wishes her hair wasn't pulled back. She feels so exposed without her hair in her face to hide behind, but she fights the urge to pull the band out.

"Hello, my name is Lara." she tells him. "Thank you for keeping me safe today."

His eyes widen with surprise, but he smiles with pleasure. "My name is Celan," he tells her in a soft but gruff voice. "It was my pleasure to guard you today, little mechanic." It seemed to her the Hissa men loved giving women nicknames. She doesn't mind this one so much, but she wants only Selon calling her *shamira.*

She turns to face Woken. He's so big that if it wasn't for Selon's solid presence behind her, she wouldn't be able to look up into his stony face without panicking.

"Thank you for guarding me, Woken. I'm sorry for all the times I've been fearful." She watches with interest as the giant's face melts into a smile, and he drops to his knees in front of her. That puts his face even with hers.

"It's been my honor just to be near you," he tells her with a voice so low it might be a mountain moving. "I know you would never choose me. I'm much too large for you. But being able to just see you, to know there are more of you out there has made my life better. I go home at night, and I don't dread the next day. I wake with hope now."

She isn't expecting such eloquence from the large warrior, and she feels tears sting her eyes. One slides down her cheek, and Woken's scale pattern pales. He quickly backs away, looking over at Selon with panic.

"She's crying. You must take her to medical now. She's hurt. I don't know what I did." Woken reaches for his communicator to call for emergency assistance.

"Easy my friend," Selon says quickly, stopping Woken before he can rain down eager males on them with a cry for help. "Humans cry sometimes when they feel strong emotions, not just pain."

Woken eyes Lara with concern. "Are you sure?"

Lara gives a watery smile and nods her head. "I'm fine, I promise. Your words made me feel happy and sad at the same time."

"I only meant to make you feel cherished," Woken explains, and his bass voice deepens even further with sincerity.

"You did," she assures him. "I hope they find more of my kind soon. You deserve a kind and loving female of your own. Not a broken one like me."

Woken cocks his head in confusion. "Why would you think you're broken? Fear doesn't mean you're broken. We all have fear. Facing fear makes you brave. Considering what you must have suffered, you must be the bravest person I've ever met. Male or female."

"I agree with Woken," Celan pipes up, turning all their attention to him. "I saw your fear yesterday when the bay was surrounded. You were so scared I could smell it. I thought they would need to medicate you before you'd be able to leave. But here you are, walking out the door on your own two feet. You smell of caution but not fear. And you speak to us. You're very brave, Lara Stray. We're proud to know you." Celan finishes his statement by standing up and solemnly tapping his finger on his chest over his heart.

With her brows furrowed; Lara starts to make the same gesture when Selon squeezes her hand to get her attention. "Men tap their heart to greet women. It's an acknowledgment that women are the heart of Hissa. If you wish to use a traditional Hissa greeting also, then tap your fingers at your neck to show that you respect that he's willing to give his life for you and Hissa," Selon explains.

Looking back to Celan, she taps her fingers to her throat, and he beams and breathes out. "I never thought to be greeted as such ever again," he says, his voice heavy with emotion.

Turning to face Woken, she repeats the gesture, and she can hear the impact as he moves with too much speed to tap his chest in response. "How do men greet each other?" she asks. Without another word, Celan and Woken face each other and touch the spot between their eyes.

"It's an acknowledgment from male to male that they are ready and able to watch and guard Hissa," Selon explains, then returns the gesture as both men do the same to him.

"If you were to greet another female, you would place a hand on your belly for a moment, and so would she. Acknowledging each other as life givers. If you're close friends, you would hold your hands low and palms out to invite the other woman to touch your belly instead of touching it yourself."

"I like that none of the greetings require touching except if invited," Lara murmurs thoughtfully. "The Gormian press the whole front of their bodies to each other as a casual greeting. It's horrible." She gives a theatrical shudder, showing everyone that she's making light of it, and they obligingly chuckle. Then her stomach growls, drawing all their gazes to her abdomen.

"Is there a little beast in there?" Celan asks blinking down at her with interest.

"Humans make that sound when they're hungry," Selon explains with a laugh.

"Then it's time to escort you home," Woken says as he brings up his data bracelet again. "I'll call a transport."

"Can we walk?" Lara asks, making them all go still.

"Of course," Selon says quickly. "If you feel confident."

"I would like to try," she says. But then, even with all her newfound confidence, she finds herself tugging the band out of her hair, so it falls back over her face. Feeling less exposed, she squeezes Selon's hand tighter and nods her head.

They start walking, Celan in front, Selon and Lara next, with Woken bringing up the rear. At first no one seems to notice. Everyone is hurrying home for the evening meal. But it's not long until glances turn into stares. Men stop moving. Then they start to gather.

Soon they're moving through the crowd that's stopped to watch her go by. Celan and Woken change places, and the giant just plows through people, forcing men to move or get stepped on. Lara feels the familiar fear building. Her heart is racing. The sun seems too bright for her eyes, and there isn't enough air to breathe.

She's made a horrible decision.

A hand reaches out for her, one of many. But this one makes it through and touches her arm.

She wants to scream. She wants to climb up on Selon and close her eyes and let the panic take her. She wants to run.

But she ignores all those impulses and makes herself look up at the man who's holding her.

"Please let go," she says in a clear but shaky voice. Everyone freezes when she speaks, and Woken turns, about to slap the man away when he withdraws at her request. The buzzing of voices trying to get her attention suddenly stops, waiting for her to speak again.

"I'm hungry and tired," she tells them. "I want to go to Tiran's house. Please let me pass."

As if her words hold magic power, the men around them step away, clearing a path for the four of them to walk comfortably. They don't disperse, but they stop trying to talk to her or touch her.

As she passes, she taps her throat and there's a constant flurry of movement as males all around her touch their chests over their hearts. Everyone's eyes are so solemn as she passes that for a moment it feels like she's part of a funeral procession.

Then she sees something else in their faces. Hope. They are solemn because just like Woken and Celan, they never thought they'd be tapping their chests to greet a female again. They're experiencing something they thought forever lost to them.

It's obvious from the expression on the men's faces that this simple exchange of greeting gestures is a profound and uplifting moment. Now she feels selfish for hiding herself away. She's going to make sure Deena and Mara know how to properly greet Hissa men. She's going to make sure that these beautiful traditional movements become common again.

"Well done," Selon whispers in her ear. "You're so brave, little *shamira*." She doesn't feel brave. Her knees feel weak, and her hands are shaking. She's not sure she can walk all the way. As if reading her mind Selon squeezes her hand. "I can carry you, but I think you can walk. One step at a time, sweet *shamira*. Just one step at a time."

It feels like she's run all day by the time they reach Tiran's house, instead of the short mile walk from the port. The door opens as they approach and Mara rushes out, folding her into a hug with tears in her eyes.

"You just walked through fire," she whispers in Lara's ear with fierce pride. "No one but my sister could be so strong!" Lara realizes Mara's been watching her. Letting her make her way with Selon and the guards. Letting her face the men.

Lara's not sure she can speak around the ball of emotion in her throat, but that doesn't matter because Mara releases her from the hug and grabs her free hand to drag her into the house.

"There's a feast waiting. Get in here and eat!" Mara looks over her shoulder at Woken and Celan. "You guys are welcome to join us too." Then she notices Lara is holding tightly to Selon's hand and dragging him along as Mara drags her. She raises her gaze to regard Selon with a half-smile. "And I'm guessing there is no way I could get her to let you go, so I hope you can eat one-handed."

Lara relaxes a little when she realizes Mara won't make Selon leave and feels lighthearted and happy as they all troop into the house.

Mara wasn't exaggerating when she claimed there was a feast waiting. Every surface of the kitchen is covered in platters of food, the smells making Lara's mouth water with hunger. Tiran and Deena are already in the kitchen. Tiran looks frustrated as he tries to find a spot to set down the platter he's holding. Deena is already filling a smaller plate full of food with gleeful delight. She looks up to see everyone enter and raises her eyebrow at Lara when she sees her gripping Selon's hand so tightly.

Lara flushes and ducks her head with a shy smile, making Deena laugh.

Tiran glares at her and the guards. "I didn't hear a transport."

"We walked," Selon volunteers. Lara decides she's been brave enough today and takes a small step back behind Selon so she can hide from Tiran's angry gaze.

"That was dangerous," Tiran growls out. To her surprise, Woken speaks up in her defense.

"There was no danger, and Lara deserves to see and be seen. She handled herself well," he tells Tiran. "Selon helped her stay calm, and she stands here now, safely before you. Don't make her fearful after enduring so much."

Tiran flushes with embarrassment. "I'm sorry," he says, and Lara assumes he was speaking to Woken until she sees him look around Selon's broad frame. "I'm so concerned with protecting you, sister. I think I might overdo the role sometimes."

"Sometimes?" Deena calls out with heavy sarcasm. Tiran shoots her a look of annoyance, but she just gives him a cheeky grin.

He looks back at Lara. "I will be better. I argued adamantly against letting you spend the night in the bay, but I see that it was good for you. I'm glad Mara was able to win me to her way of thinking."

"Yeah, about that," Deena pipes up. "I need my own place. You guys do everything loud. Argue, fuck, everything. It's getting old."

Mara looks over to Deena with a deep blush and a little gasp. "That's rude to just yell across a room!"

Deena gives an unconcerned shrug. "But true."

Lara's able to relax as Deena draws everyone's attention to herself, getting into a verbal sparring match with both Tiran and Mara. She knows Deena did it on purpose and shoots her friend a grateful look.

"How about some dinner?" Selon asks and moves them toward the food, ignoring the arguing going on around them. She looks at their intertwined hands and then at his face.

"I'm going to let go of your hand," she tells him with a small smile. "But I reserve the right to grab onto it again."

"Any time you wish," he promises.

They both find plates, fill them with food, then sit down in the living room. They're soon joined by Celan and Woken, but Tiran, Mara, and Deena stay in the kitchen to argue while they eat.

"All three of them are noisy," Woken grunts.

Lara stifles a laugh. "This is them being pretty mild," she tells them, and all three men look at her with horror.

"You live with this, all the time?" Celan asks.

"Well, no," Lara feels obligated to point out. "Tiran and Mara spend a lot of time having loud sex and Deena spends a lot of time on communicators yelling at the insurance company trying to get them to pay for Ally. The three of them aren't always loud. Occasionally they sleep."

"Why does she need them to pay?" Selon asks. "She shouldn't be in want of anything here on Hissa."

"She says it's the principle of the thing," Lara explains with a dismissive shrug. "We paid high premiums for years, and she wants something to show for it. There was one month we lived on stale meal bars because that's all we could afford after fuel and the premium payment."

"I think she might like to cause discord," Woken rumbles. "She could find trouble in an empty field."

"I've heard that," Celan agrees, then grins. "But who would want a tame female, eh? It would take all the fun out of it." The men laugh, and Lara lets the conversation flow around her, content to sit and eat with Selon's warm body next to hers.

She's surprised to find herself relaxed, sitting and eating with so many men in the room. She knows part of it is Selon. He makes her feel confident, and he gives her strength. But more than that, she doesn't feel the deep instinct she's had for so long. There's no need to run and hide. She doesn't feel the familiar panic sitting deep in her belly, just waiting to bloom. There's a warm contentedness filling her instead.

Eventually, a canister of himora, a spicy alcohol and a Hissa favorite, is passed around. Lara doesn't touch it, and Mara and Deena only sip, but the men throw it back by the cupful.

"I forgot to tell you," Tiran suddenly says. He's sitting in a large pillow stuffed chair with Mara cuddled in his lap. "We've managed to trace the sales of several Decanted women. One was sold to an Anavac family as a pet, and a ship is being deployed to pick her up.

"I'll be on that ship," Woken rumbles out proudly and casts a quick glance over at Mara. "Thank you for putting in a good word for me."

"It's the least I could do," Mara says with a sassy grin. "You were a really good sport about our battle in front of the Council."

"I've never been so glad to lose," Woken says with a smirk, making everyone chuckle. Lara's heard about the fight between Woken and Mara held in front of the Council so Mara could prove she wasn't held against her will by Tiran. Now she wonders if Woken might not have used all his skills and strength during the fight with Mara

"You said one was sold. Have you found where others are?" Deena says, bringing the focus back on Tiran.

"We've found a bill of sale for her to the pleasure ship Delight. There's already a small team deployed. If she is still there, they will retrieve her and bring her back."

"Pleasure ship?" Lara asks, fearful that it's as bad as it sounds. Mara shakes her head quickly.

"Pleasure ships aren't brothels. They have gambling, shops, dining, entertainment, and stuff like that. So many civilizations have much stricter rules for brothels that pleasure ships don't bother with that form of entertainment. Ships like the Delight travel to planets and stay there for a month or two, then move onto the next planet." She looks over to Tiran. "Do we know what she was sold for? What purpose?"

He shakes his head. "No, but we can see that she was requested to be strong and athletic. Perhaps a performer? She was Decanted at the biological age of six and shipped off. The records are old, but we think she's still there."

"Our males will find her," Woken rumbles. "They'll bring her back and make her safe, as we did with you three."

"Hey, I wasn't unsafe," Mara objects.

Lara gives a little sigh. This is a common argument between Mara and almost every Hissa. She knows the next step is for Deena to jump in and start asking to pilot shuttles because she's bored, or maybe start an argument about the difference between protecting and smothering.

Instead, Deena gives her a concerned look. "You're looking pretty tired over there," she comments, drawing everyone's attention to Lara. She blushes a little and ducks her head.

"I guess I am," she admits. "A lot has happened in the last two days." With a full stomach and a safe feeling in her heart, her body is ready to sleep.

"Who is on guard tonight?" Tiran asks.

"It's us until second moon rise," Celan answers. "Then Sarin and Titin replace us."

Tiran nods, satisfied with their answer. Smiling and teasing each other about falling asleep during guard duty, Celan and Woken move to take their posts just outside the entrance. Selon stands and turns to Lara. Her heart stutters a little at the thought of him leaving. She assumed he'd stay and share her bed again, but the look on his face makes her think that might not happen.

He looks like he's waiting for her to say something. *Do I ask him to stay*?

She looks around and with all eyes on her, she's not sure what to tell them. She knows Tiran and Mara won't like the idea, and Deena will tease her mercilessly, not realizing how much it hurts Lara when she does.

Is she ready to face them to keep Selon with her?

She looks back at his face and with a small smile of regret he shakes his head.

"You've done enough today," he tells her. "You've been brave enough. Wait until tomorrow to be brave again."

He bids everyone good evening and leaves.
Lara feels her heart break a little as he strides out the door.

CHAPTER

14

Selon stares at his ceiling. He's been doing that since he went to bed. All he can do is lie there and think of Lara. Think of her lying next to him. Remembering the smell of her. He desperately wants to go back to Tiran's house and demand entrance, but he can't. Lara needs to make that decision. Learn to voice her demands. He can't do it for her.

Knowing that doesn't make it any easier to remain lying in his big, empty, round bed.

Frustrated, he rolls over so at least now he's staring at his wall instead of the ceiling. The new view doesn't help. With a curse he gets up, deciding if he can't sleep, he might as well do some reading. He doesn't bother turning on any lights as he shuffles to the main room of his small house. He finds his large data pad and settles down into a comfortable chair to read the latest results for samples taken from Mara, Deena, and the ones flown in from Mian. Too worried about traumatizing Lara, none of the scientists requested samples from her after she visited medical when she first arrived.

He also reads the short report on the Decanted female who was stolen from Emerion Station. One of their battleships reached the station not long after she went missing. In hopes of finding her quickly, several more ships are being sent to investigate the inhabited areas around Emerion Station.

A small sound draws his attention from his reading. Putting down his data pad, he looks around the darkened room. Listening carefully, he hears it again coming from the bedroom. His small house is only one story and the bedroom and bath are all one large room. The food preparation area is separated from the main room by only a low wall.

He walks silently to the door. It could be one of the small creatures that roam his half-wild garden. It's happened before where one of the little beasts decided to explore the inside of the house. He's spent so much time on the moons or with the military that he's come home several times to find nests among his rafters or burrows under his bed. Each time he extracted the animal with no harm done, except for once when he gave up his bedroom to a family of tillintails, waiting patiently for the babies to grow large enough to follow their parents out his front door. Even if they left a horrible mess and bad smell, they'd made him smile.

Maybe, if another breeding pair are moving in, he'll leave them so Lara can see. He knows she'll enjoy watching the babies grow. The small, scaled creatures are generally harmless, and their young are adorable. Not to mention, they're considered a sign of good luck.

His window is wide open. Like most other Hissa men, he never bothers to lock down his house unless a particularly violent storm hits. But tonight, the sky is clear, and Diminish is high in the sky, casting a soft light through the window and to the floor near his bed. He hears the sound again. This time he's able to zero in on the wide-open window. He waits, expecting to see the narrow head of a tillintail appear.

No scaly head appears. What he does see freezes him in place. With absolute astonishment, he watches Lara's lithe body climb in through the high set window. Dropping effortlessly to the floor with a soft sigh of satisfaction, she turns to the bed and starts to get in slowly, as if trying not to disturb someone already in the bed. When she realizes it's empty, she makes a frustrated sound and throws the covers aside.

"You could have come through the front door," he says. At his words, she screams and jumps out of his bed. Whirling around, she covers her heart with her hand and takes a few deep breaths.

"Selon! I think my heart just shifted in my chest," she complains and then gives him a big smile. "You're here. I worried the empty bed meant you were somewhere else, or I had the wrong house."

"Correct house and correct bed," he says and strides forward with open arms. She eagerly moves into his embrace, snuggles against him, and makes a deep contented sound.

"This is nice," she murmurs. "I know it hasn't been long, but I missed you, and I couldn't sleep. I thought about going to the port and climbing the communication tower but decided to climb you instead."

"I approve," he tells her quickly. "But how did you know this was my house?"

"That's easy. I asked Woken. He drew the map for me."

It's so simple he blinks. He expected her to tell an elaborate story of stealing a data pad or subtly questioning Tiran. It didn't occur to him that she would just outright ask. For now, he knows she's not ready to face the consequences of everyone knowing they're intimate. Asking for the location of his house would've been highly suspicious and might've led to a conversation she's not ready to have. "Did he wonder why you wanted to know where I lived?"

"No, because I also asked him where everyone I know lives, and he added them to the map." She pulls away from him so she can tug a piece of memory paper out of her pocket and shows him. "I told them it's important for me to learn Hissa geography and where all my friends' homes are located."

A surprisingly detailed sketch of the area shows not only his house but also the houses of Penon, Woken, Celan, Sarin, and Tiran. Tiran's house is marked as a reference as well as several tram lines and the port at the city center. "Woken is very good," he comments as he studies the map.

"He sketches too," Lara volunteers.

Selon looks up from the map. "Has he offered to draw your image, my *shamira*?"

For some reason that question makes her blush. "Yes, but I declined. He said I need to sit still or let him take a capture of me. I wasn't comfortable with either."

"Maybe someday," Selon says with a causal shrug, ignoring the strange surge of jealousy he feels at the idea of Woken drawing Lara. He's going to need to learn to share her with all of Hissa because at some point, the Council will expect her to start meeting and interacting with men.

That thought fills him with dread.

To distract himself, he pulls her back into his arms. "You got Woken to draw you a map and decided to come for a visit in the middle of the night. Should I assume no one at the house knows you're here?"

"You assume correctly," she says, twining her arms around his waist and holding him tightly. "I couldn't sleep, so I decided I needed to get out. And I thought I might test the efficacy of Woken's map by finding your bed."

That makes him bark out a laugh. "You're welcome in my home or on my body any time you wish," he tells her. "Are you hungry or fatigued, sweet *shamira*? I have food and a warm bed to offer you."

"I'm not hungry or tired," she says with confidence. He can't believe how much she's blossomed in such a short time. Maybe he should talk to her about what happened on the way home from the port. Or how well she handled Tiran once she got home. But her next words drive all thoughts out of his head.

"I'd like to have sex again," she tells him boldly, then kisses him. He feels blood start pounding through his body, and he's instantly hard inside the soft confines of his sleeping pants.

"It's my pleasure to fulfill your every desire," he tells her honestly and the smile she rewards him with is full of joy. Lifting her up, he kisses her again, enjoying the way she wraps her legs around his waist. With two strides he's at the bed, laying them both down. Although he never expected her to have the courage to seek him out, he's glad he followed the urge to use his most colorful and soft bedding. Pulling back a little, he's taken by the sight of her beautiful face framed by the deep rich burnt orange of the covers under her.

"Can I put my mouth on you again?" he asks, finding he craves the taste of her.

"Yes!" she agrees and starts pulling clothes off. "And I want to sit on you again. I want to be on top with you inside of me. I liked that. Deena said to try it a different way. I should face your feet instead. I'm not sure I want to do that. I like being able to see your eyes. But maybe we could attempt it some other time."

"Deena gave you suggestions about sex?" he inquires as he pulls off his clothes, greedily taking in her naked flesh with hungry eyes.

"She gives everyone suggestions about everything," Lara tells him with a roll of her eyes. She's kneeling on the bed now, looking eager and impatient.

The moment he's naked, she grabs hold of his arm and pulls him onto the bed. Letting her topple him into the big bed, he lands with a grunt. She flings herself onto him and starts wantonly rubbing herself against him.

"I like this," she tells him, a little breathless. He can feel her skin starting to heat, and her pupils are dilated, all indications that not only is she here of her own free will, but she's doing something she finds great pleasure in.

"I have no objections," he teases. "I seem to like to be mauled and thrown around by you." She gives a small laugh and stops moving her hips for a moment so she can bend down to kiss him.

He loses himself in the kiss, so he doesn't realize what she's doing right away when she grabs his rigid member. It's only as he feels her shift her position, so his head is poised at her entrance that he understands what she's about to do and panics a little.

"No, my sweet *shamira*. I'm not sure you're ready for that yet." He reaches to pull her hand away, but she tightens on his engorged shaft.

"I'm sure I'm ready," she insists and slides herself down a little more. "This is how to have sex. I know it is. I've talked to Deena and watched videos to make sure I don't do anything wrong. This isn't like before. I want this. I know it'll feel good. Please, Selon, please?"

As she talks, she rubs her hand up and down his shaft. Her touch causes him to moan and forget what she's begging for. He's forced to pull her strong, skilled hand away so he can think clearly.

"We don't have to," he insists. "We can use our hands and mouths, just like before. Wasn't that pleasurable? There's no need for penetration."

She pouts down at him. "I know that. I don't feel forced or coerced, Selon. This is you. You're the most trustworthy male I know. You're safe. And you make me feel things I've never felt before. I don't feel like I have to do this. I want to." She tugs at his grip on her hand, and he lets go with a groan.

"I don't want my touch to ever hurt you," he says.

"I know," she answers, her face confident without a hint of fear or anxiety. "That's why I'm here. That's why I want this. You're the one. The one to show me how it's supposed to be."

Her words fill him with elation. His chest swells with emotions, and his heart thunders in his chest. "Take anything you want from me," he answers. "Take as much or as little. Begin and stop if you wish. Anything and everything is yours."

"Thank you, Selon," she whispers, leaning over to grace him with a gentle kiss. Then she grabs his throbbing cock in her tight grip and starts easing her sex down on him.

She's tight and when he's only a quarter of the way in, he feels her tense. "Easy," he whispers and moves his hand between her legs. His fingers find her clit and he starts stroking. "We'll fit," he promises. "But we have to go slow and make your body eager for me."

"It doesn't hurt," she breathes. "You just feel so big that if I force it, then it will be painful."

"No forcing," he agrees and keeps rubbing. Then he moves another hand up to her breast. He doesn't rush, just moves his hands on her flesh in a way he knows she likes. His hips want to move, to thrust himself into her warm wetness, but he keeps his lower body still. He will keep himself under control. He will make this a good experience for her.

Slowly, she starts to relax. Her sex opens, and experimentally she pushes her hips down. She feels unbelievably hot and tight around him, but by the way she moans, it must feel as good to her as it does for him. She continues to slide down his shaft with a tortuously slow pace.

"This feels good. This is good," she murmurs and closes her eyes and sinks down until he fills her. She clenches around him, and it's all Selon can do to keep from roaring because the pleasure of it is so intense. He focuses on his own hands and movement, desperate to keep from spilling his seed before she's satisfied. She undulates against him, pulling away from him only a little then slamming back down with a shocked cry of pleasure. She does it several more times, panting and sweating with the effort, clumsy with need.

"Selon, please help me," she begs, and he realizes she can't get a rhythm to reach climax. He sits up and pulls his legs under him. She drops back to the bed with a little surprised sound and wraps her legs around his waist.

"Don't stop!" she cries out.

"I'm not stopping," he promises her. "Loosen your legs a little, sweet *shamira*. I promise not to pull away." She lets her legs relax enough so he can pull their pelvises apart. He pushes back into her, and her body spasms a little around his hard cock. He moves one hand between their bodies again, finding that nub of nerve endings he knows will be sensitive and needy by now.

"Yes, like that," she pants and grabs at him, her heels

digging into his backside. "But faster."

He increases his pace, balancing on his knees so he can reach one hand out to roll her nipple with his fingers, and with his other hand he works his thumb against her clit. She's screaming after only a few more thrusts, clenching around him with enough strength to be painful and he finds he can't hold back any longer. With a roar he's just barely able to mute, he climaxes with her, feeling his seed pour into her with pleasure so intense it feels close to pain.

"Moons preserve me," he mumbles as he collapses on the bed next to her.

She cuddles close to him, throwing an arm and leg over him, and within moments she's asleep. Feeling more satisfied than he ever thought possible, he wraps a loose arm around her and lets his own eyes close.

CHAPTER 15

Watching through her window with a big smile on her face, Lara sees Selon disappear into the night. His stride long, his body tall and confident. No longer able to see her lover, she throws herself onto her bare bed. All the bedding is in the closet, but for the first time in a long time, she doesn't feel the need to sleep in the closet. She feels sated, happy, and brave. Tonight, she might sleep in her bed instead of the floor, ensconced in a small storage space.

Rolling onto her back, she hugs herself with glee and knows she's smiling like a fool. Selon makes her feel so free. Free from anxiety. Free from fear. Free to dream of a future where she doesn't feel the need to hide all the time.

She feels so bold that she decides she'll demand to have her own place sometime soon. That will be the first step. Getting a place where she can find the type of quiet she needs. With access to engines and parts, she can set up several systems in her own home that will make noise to cover the strange quiet that exists on most of Hissa. Then, once the house is situated just the way she likes it, she'll invite Selon to visit her. He might even spend the whole night. She could even ask him to move in with her. It could be her space with Selon there.

To her, that sounds like a slice of heaven.

I'll talk to Mara tomorrow, she thinks, making her heartbeat speed up a little with excitement. *I'll ask for a home of my own. I'll make it perfect, then show it to Selon.*

That makes her wonder what kind of things Selon likes. His house was very bare. Except for the colorful blankets on the bed, there was almost no color anywhere and minimal possessions. He probably doesn't like a lot of clutter. Well, she can make sure to ask for a place with several rooms so she can keep all her tools and parts in one room, out of the way. That would keep the rest of the house neat and tidy.

Oh, and she can ask for bright blankets just like the ones Selon has. That would make him feel at home. She's so eager to make this happen that she's tempted to go wake up Mara and Tiran. Almost.

No, she'll need to wait until tomorrow. She looks back to the window to gaze at Brimming lighting up the sky and hiding all but the brightest stars. She could've spent the night with Selon. He woke her and offered her a choice. Either use a communicator and wake up Tiran and Mara so they would know where she is and wouldn't think she'd been kidnapped or let him escort her home before the household woke and found her missing.

Unwilling to face a grumpy Tiran awoken from a peaceful sleep, she'd opted to return. Sneaking back in the same way she left.

But now she regrets that decision. Could she just leave them a note and go back to Selon's house? She could make sure to leave the note someplace obvious, so no one would worry. Then she'd be free to spend the night cuddling up with a warm and wonderful Selon.

That makes her think about bedding down with Selon every night. Having him always there. Now that she's gotten a taste of him, she can't imagine life without him. His deep, calm voice in her ear. The feel of his skin against her. His gentle closed mouth smiles. His bright, expressive eyes.

It became clear to her very quickly that all of Hissa is waiting for her to pick a male. Well, she's chosen and couldn't be happier. Now all she has to do is make everyone aware of her choice.

Tiran might push back, but he probably wouldn't be happy with any choice. He's a picky, prickly bastard. But Mara loves him, and Lara knows he does it out of an overabundance of caution. She'll put up with his bad mood and objections. Besides, she knows Mara and Deena will back up any decisions she makes. Especially Deena, who's been encouraging her to explore with Selon.

As she stares at Brimming and thinks about all this, a face appears in her window, making her freeze with fear. The unfamiliar Hissa grins at her, making her eyes go wide with shock. Who is this, and what does he think he's doing?

Then he does the unthinkable: he climbs in through her open window. Heart in her throat, she launches herself off the bed and flings herself to the door, mouth open to scream. Before she can even draw in a lung full of air, the man tackles her from behind, knocking her to the floor and pinning her there with his bulk.

He doesn't say anything; he just works quickly. He shoves a gag in her mouth and secures it behind her head. She tries to bite it, but the rubber ball is resistant to her teeth. The tightness of it around her head tells her she's not going to be able to just rub it off.

She scrabbles her hands around the floor, trying to find anything to use as a weapon. There's nothing there, and the man easily grabs first one hand and then the other to secure behind her back. She moans with fear and adrenaline floods her system. The man gets off her and pivots on his knees so he can grab her ankles, binding them as well. Then he stands and picks her up, throwing her over his shoulder. Without much effort, he climbs out the window and down a collapsible ladder.

She struggles, knowing that once the adrenaline wears off, her body will shut down and she'll be too weak to escape. The man grunts at her struggles but doesn't even pause. He just secures her with both arms and starts running. Tears begin pouring out of her eyes, and the hard jostle of her stomach against his shoulder makes it hard for her to breathe.

She's not sure how long or how far they run until the man finally stops and enters a house. The place is dark, but that doesn't slow him. He strides up some stairs and through another room. She hears a door shut.

"Engage locks," he tells the house, and her heart sinks as she hears the door and windows lock. "Lights on." The room lights up, and Lara blinks her eyes with the sudden brightness.

"I'm sorry," he tells her as he gently lays her out on a bed. She looks around and sees she's in a bedroom. The large round bed and clothes stacked in a corner tells her it's probably his room. She looks over and sees the window has been covered by a dark film on the outside. She won't be able to signal anyone for help.

Looking back at him, she tries to plead with her eyes. *Please let me go. Please don't do this.*

"I didn't want to steal you away," he tells her and kneels on the floor next to the bed, putting his face close to hers. "I asked so many times to meet you, but they kept telling me you weren't ready. That I had to be patient. That I had to wait. But I couldn't wait any longer."

He points to the stack of clothes. "Those are all for you. I had them made to your measurements. The health report sent out by the Council included your size. All of these clothes I had made for you just arrived yesterday. You'll love them. I picked every one of them. All of them are beautiful colors and made from the softest of fabrics." He reaches out to stroke her face, and she jerks away from his touch with a moan of despair, muffled by the gag.

"You stink of fear," he tells her and wrinkles his nose in distaste. "You don't need to be afraid. I'd never hurt you. I only want to care for you. I'll go slow. I'll only touch you with my hands until you are ready to accept me inside you." He draws his hand away from her. "But we can't wait too long. It can take over a week for mating marks to appear, and I don't want them to find you until your skin is marked from my touch."

His words make Lara pull herself into a ball and shake. He just told her he's going to rape her. Back before the Great Death took all the Hissa women and devastated the male population, men and women got together for what they called the Knowledge Period.

Young couples who thought they might like to enter into a Family Pact would live together for several weeks. Knowledge Period is a time for all kinds of interactions, including sex. If the couple were biologically compatible, a design, unique to each couple, would appear around the woman's neck and shoulders. Mara developed the marks with Tiran. Now this stranger wants to see if he can make marks appear on her neck.

The marks didn't always mean that a couple would enter into a Family Pact, and the lack of mating marks didn't mean the couple wouldn't stay together. But mating marks are considered signs of fertility and a good pairing. With both Mian and Mara developing them, the marks took on an almost sacred status.

The stranger wants to force her into coupling with him just to see his marks appear.

If I'm going to wear any man's marks, she thinks fiercely, *they'll be Selon's, not yours, you piece of waste.* She tries to wiggle away from him, but he just grabs a hip and pulls her back toward his side of the bed.

"Please don't move away from me. You must accustom yourself to my touch." He reaches up to start running his hand down her hair and ignores her when she flinches away from him.

"My name's Nonin. I'm training to be a rock diver on Diminish. I'll be very good when I'm finished with my apprenticeship," he tells her eagerly while he runs his hands through her hair. She can tell he's trying to be gentle, but unlike Selon's skilled fingers, his catch and tangle in her black hair.

"I know my hands are rough from labor, but I'll work on making them soft for you. Soft, just like your hair." He leans forward, his eyes dreamy and she thinks he's going to kiss her but instead he sniffs along her head and to her neck.

He violently draws away and glares down at her. His blue scale pattern turns black with anger. "You have the smell of another male on you." He starts running his nose over her, smelling her clothing and bared forearms. "This won't do!" he declares and starts ripping at her clothes. She tries to scream behind the gag, but it just comes out as a mewling noise. Soon she's laying naked, her clothes torn and tossed outside the bedroom door. He looks down at her, still frowning.

"I can still smell him on you. I'm sorry, but you need to be bathed." He picks her up and carries her to the bathroom, laying her down on the cold floor. He reaches over and turns on a faucet, fiddling with it until he's satisfied, and then slides her under the running water. She gasps as he starts pouring cleaning gel all over her body and rubbing it into a lather with a rough cloth.

He stops and leans in closer to her chest, holding her still with a large hand against her stomach. "Your skin is so delicate. You have red patches where I've scrubbed. I'm afraid I'm being much too rough." He stands abruptly and strides off, uncaring about the wet trail he's making as his clothes are now soaked.

She struggles while he's gone, trying to loosen the binding around her wrists and ankles, but if anything, the water seems to be making them tighter. She looks around wildly, hoping to see something she can use to cut them. Except for a few towels and a bottle of cleanser, there's nothing in the bathroom except her.

Then some of the soap slides down her side and pools under the small of her back. It's slick and she works her hands through it, coating her bonds in the slippery substance. She can feel the bindings moving now and is just about to slide a hand free when Nonin returns. She goes still, afraid he might notice that one of her hands is starting to slip loose of the binding.

"I'm have something better to wash you with," he announces and holds up a small square of cloth. He starts to scrub her again, scouring every inch of her. His touch isn't sexual. The scale pattern on his head is a deep blue, not purple, as he rubs every part of her to get Selon's scent off. When he's done, he closes his eyes, leans in close, and sniffs.

"I don't smell him anymore," he pronounces with a smile and sits back on his heels. He opens his eyes, and Lara can't help the whimper that comes out of her. His face is full of lust, and his scale pattern has turned a deep shade of purple. She tries to wiggle away from him, but he easily scoops her up and carries her dripping wet to the bed.

"I'll take such good care of you," he tells her, and he briskly dries her. "I want to take you hiking in the jungle. There's a beautiful place I want to show you. There's a waterfall and grotto."

I'm not my fear, she reminds herself. The panic tries to overwhelm her again as he dries her breasts. She pictures Selon's face in her mind, his words, his steadiness and kindness. What would he say to her? Yes, she can just hear his words in her mind: *you're stronger than your fear. You're so much stronger than you think you are.*

Once she's dry, he tosses the cloth aside and just gazes down at her. *He's going to rape me now,* she thinks.

Suddenly, she's not afraid anymore. She's angry.

They all promised to keep her safe. They promised it would always be her choice. Rage fills her. Tiran, Mara, the Council, the guards, the whole damn planet. All of them promised nothing like this would happen.

Betrayal fills her. The Hissa gave her Selon and made her feel safe. Then suddenly and brutally all the security is torn away. Her freedom is stripped from her like the clothing Nonin ripped from her body.

He reaches for her legs, untying the restraints there, but before she can kick at him, he's putting his body between her legs, holding her securely with his arms. "No, please don't fight," he tells her softly, leaning his face close to her sex. "I'm just going to taste you. I won't take you before you're ready, but I do need a taste."

She wonders if he can see the hate in her eyes as she glares at him and shakes her head.

Pounding at the door makes him sit up and curse.

"Nonin, open this door! Right now! Open it!" a voice bellows. She doesn't recognize the voice but feels intense relief when Nonin stiffens and looks away from her. "Who could this be? I'm on break for another two months. They can't force me back to the moon so soon."

He pulls away from her, giving her a quick kiss on the cheek before he gets off the bed and stands up. Looking down at her with deep affection, he smiles. "Stay, sweet, lovely female. I'll be right back to care for you."

He runs out of the room to confront the person at the door just as she hears a massive crash. Wasting no time, she pulls frantically at her wrists, feeling her flesh tear as she works herself free. Without even pausing to find clothing, she lunges to a nearby window, breaking fingernails as she scrabbles for the latch.

She moans with relief when she finds the window isn't locked any longer. She doesn't know why the house locks disengaged, but without hesitation, she pushes the window open and climbs out, taking the single-story fall with ease. She hits the ground running. She can feel the rough ground biting at her feet and the jungle tearing at her naked body, but she can't stop. Fear, rage, and adrenaline push her hard, urging her faster and faster into the dense dark jungle.

She's not sure how long she's been running or how many miles she manages to cover before she starts to feel the adrenaline bleeding out of her system. She knows this sensation well. Soon her legs will feel like lead. Her eyes won't want to stay open. She'll end up lying down wherever she's standing. Both she and her sister suffer from the same error in their genetic makeup. An adrenaline crash sends them into a coma-like sleep.

She needs to find a place to hide from Nonin before that happens.

She slows to a walk, trying to hear the world around her, attempting to sense if Nonin is nearby. She can't make out anything but the sound of the jungle and her own wild heartbeat. She's warm now, but knows she'll grow cold soon. She gets on her hands and knees, searching in the darkness for a place to curl up and sleep.

She finds a hollow under some thick vines, right next to a recently fallen tree. She digs until it's just large enough for her to curl up in. Once inside, she pulls vines over the opening, effectively hiding her. She can feel things crawling on her skin and the ground feels horribly cold, but her eyes are closing, and she can't fight the lethargy any longer.

I'll be strong again tomorrow, she tells herself, too tired to even cry now. *I'll find Selon, and he'll help me be strong again.*

CHAPTER

16

Unable to keep the smile off his face, Selon takes his time turning away from Lara's darkened window. It's a nice night, and now both moons are high in the sky. He should be tired but feels nothing but elation. Everything seems to be crisper to his senses. The night smells richer to his nose, the light of the moons more brilliant, the night animals and bugs seem to be singing songs of happiness.

He's about halfway home when something doesn't feel right. He's not sure why, but the feeling makes him stop in his tracks and turn back toward Tiran's house. Lara's safe, he tells himself. There are guards at her door. Tiran's in the house and ever vigilant. And Deena's in the room right next to hers. Besides, this is Hissa. No male would dare hurt her.

But if recent events at the port are taken into consideration, the Council's decree to give Lara space isn't necessarily working.

And then he thinks about all the men he's counseled over the years. Men so desperate they consider suicide. Men so lonely and unfulfilled they agree to dangerous space missions in hopes of dying in combat because suicide is so dishonorable. That kind of desperation could drive a male to do something not only illegal but against the very heart of Hissa society.

Deciding there's no harm in doubling back and just checking in on Lara, he turns and starts jogging back to the house. His disquiet just keeps growing as he gets closer, and by the time he sees the house, he's sprinting back to her window. That same window is wide open, and he can't remember if he saw her close it after she climbed through. With an easy leap he lands on the window ledge and jumps inside, already seeing the signs of a struggle before his feet hit the bedroom floor.

"She's missing," he bellows to the house, turning on the lights and slamming the bedroom door open. "Lara's missing! She's gone! She's been taken!"

The house comes alive as he tries to smell the male who took her. The scent isn't familiar, but he's having a hard time because he can also smell the acrid sent of Lara's fear permeating the room. Then Sarin and Titin, two guards from the front rush in at the same time as a sleepy Deena, a confused Mara, and an enraged Tiran join him.

"What are you doing in my house at this hour?" Tiran roars at Selon.

"Explanations later!" Selon roars right back at him. "Lara isn't here. Smell! You can smell her terror."

Tiran takes a deep breath through his nose and lets out a cry of rage, making Deena jump.

"We need to find her," Mara gasps. "Who the hell would take her?"

"Any desperate male," Sarin responds grimly.

"They wouldn't . . ." Deena starts, and for the first time since meeting her, Selon watches her flounder, at a loss for words.

"Rape her?" Mara bites out. "Yes, someone might." She points to her mating marks. "They want this. They want their seed to make this happen. The woman doesn't have to be willing, just present."

Deena pales. "That would break her. I don't think her mind would make it through that. She was so broken when I found her. Just a shell. She was just so . . ." A choked sob comes out of her, the confident and sarcastic Deena missing, replaced by a woman in so much distress she can't quite think.

Titin steps into the room and sniffs. "I don't recognize the male. Sarin?"

"I don't either," Sarin responds quickly. "We need Penon. He's the best tracker we have." He turns to tap his communicator, and Selon moves to the window, jumping out the way he came in. He examines the ground, hoping to find tracks, even knowing this isn't his strong suit, but he needs to do something.

Soon Penon is there, calm and ready. "I need something of hers with a strong smell," he demands, and Tiran rushes to hand him a piece of her bedding. When Penon breathes deep, Selon has to control the urge to rip the scrap of fabric away from him, to shield even her scent from other males.

Penon starts slow, sniffing the fabric, then the air, then the fabric again. Everyone stays back, trying to keep their scents from muddying the trail. Selon wants to scream at the man to hurry. Demand he move faster. Lara is out there, being held and hurt while Penon takes tentative steps around Tiran's house.

Then suddenly Penon is running. They all hurry to follow, and Selon struggles to keep his distance, knowing Penon needs the advantage of clear air to pick up the faint traces of Lara. Every few strides, Penon stops, sniffs, then starts running again. The halting progress makes Selon want to tear into everyone around him. This feeling of desperation is new to him and tests his iron control.

Finally, Penon leads them to the front door of a house. He stands at the door for a second, smelling deeply, then turns to them with a bleak expression. "Here," he says simply and jumps out of the way as Selon throws his body at the door at the same time as Sarin yells out for the occupant to open up the house.

The house is locked down, and the door secured, so when Tiran puts his weight against it with Selon, it just starts to creak. When Sarin and Titin join in, they are able to burst it open, the middle of the door caving in from their combined strength. The locks disengaging only as the breach triggers an emergency alarm.

"Get away!" a man says, running toward them. "She's mine. Get away!"

He barrels into Titin, knocking the man over. Selon reaches out and grabs the stranger by the shirt, swinging him around, punching the side of the man's head with his other hand, but the blow doesn't even phase him.

"Mine!" the man growls and throws a punch back at Selon, catching him in the face.

Selon staggers and roars back. Lunging at the man, he drives his shoulder into his opponent's sternum. They trade blows, neither giving nor gaining ground. Selon knows he's taking damage, but his rage is too great to feel it. This man stole his Lara. This man hurt his Lara. Her scent is all over him. Her fear. Her terror.

Grabbing the man by his head, ignoring the punches to his ribs, Selon viciously and violently brings the man's face down to his knee and feels fierce joy when he hears cartilage break. The man groans and slumps. He looks up, ready to find and care for Lara only to see Mara rushing back into the room.

"She's gone," she calls out. "The window's open, and there are knotted ropes covered in blood on the bed. I think she got loose and ran."

"I'm on it!" Penon calls and runs out of the house and around the side where the open window is located. Everyone rushes to follow as he starts tracking again. It's not long before they are deep in the jungle, following Lara's scent far from any regular trails.

They spend hours hiking through the jungle. Both moons fade away as the sun rises, but they still haven't found her.

"This is very bad," Titin mutters, and Selon scowls at him.

"You don't think I know that? You don't think we all know that?" Selon explodes, finding he can't contain his terror for Lara's safety any longer.

The jungle can be dangerous to even an experienced Hissa. A frightened woman with no skills and no equipment doesn't stand much of a chance. It's rare, but Hissa have gotten so lost in the planet's vast jungle that they disappear, never to be seen again.

It's not long before dawn breaks, and Penon starts to mutter to himself about the heat creating too many competing smells. Selon realizes that Lara's scent must be getting fainter as Penon starts to move slower and slower through the dense jungle.

"Lara!" Selon calls out suddenly. "It's Selon, please come out! You're safe now. No one's going to hurt you."

As soon as he starts calling, everyone else does too. He stops Titin and Sarin from adding their voices. "Don't call to her," he tells them. "She doesn't know you as well. Let Tiran, Deena, Mara, and myself call." They nod stiffly and remain silent.

Abruptly, Penon comes to a halt. He does a small circle. Everyone goes quiet, and they all move quickly, getting out of his way. After a few passes, his face contorts in frustration, and he looks up at them.

"I've lost her trail. I don't know what happened. Her scent has just disappeared."

Before Selon can demand Penon try again. Or scream at the male not to give up, movement out of the corner of his eye makes him freeze. Slowly, he turns to see a small hand emerge from under some vines.

"Selon?"

The voice is so soft he almost thinks he's imagined it. He scrambles over and digs his hands into the vines, finding a warm, naked body. He pulls carefully, and Lara emerges. He hears gasps and questions behind him, but ignores them all, his entire being is focused on the dirty, naked, shaking woman in his arms.

"Moons preserve me," Penon curses. "She crawled into minoli vines. No wonder I lost the scent. Those things cover everything's scent. The animals use them to hide. I might have never found her."

Selon ignores him, his full concentration on Lara. The moment he has her free of the plants, she wraps her trembling body around him. "Don't let go," she whispers to him, her eyes shut tight. "Don't ever let go."

"No," he promises without hesitation. "I'll never let go."

CHAPTER

17

As he carries her, Selon strokes Lara's back. The dense green canopy keeps the sun from lighting up her skin, but he can still see every bruise and mark on her. Walking on either side of him, Deena and Mara talk to her, but she won't respond. She keeps her long legs wrapped around his waist and her arms around his neck like bands of steel. And she refuses to lift her face from where it's buried in his neck. Her quiet sobs make him want to find Nonin and pull each limb from that male's body. Every tear that soaks into his shirt feels like a physical blow, and it's all Selon can do to keep his words calm and soothing.

Following Penon's unerring guidance, the group finds their way out of the jungle, popping out at a trail head between two clusters of houses. With a scowl and a grunt, Tiran takes over and leads the group to his house. Selon doesn't approve of going back there. This is the same house she was abducted from, and it might have an adverse effect on her mental health. Or she might find it comforting to be back in a familiar place. He reserves judgment, willing to let Lara's reaction guide him.

When they reach Tiran's front door Lara looks up and shakes her head violently.

"No," she moans, just loud enough for him and the two women standing next to him to hear. "Not here. No." Selon freezes at her words, unsure what to do.

"What's wrong now?" Tiran asks, his voice loud and heavy with displeasure. "We need to get her inside and comfortable. See to her wounds and assess her health. Why are you hesitating, Selon?"

"She doesn't want to go back in there," Selon explains calmly as he glares at Tiran. Trying to convey his frustration at Tiran with his expression, even as he keeps his voice even and pleasant. "And you need to quiet your voice and temper."

"I need to see to Lara's well-being," Tiran retorts, his voice just as loud and harsh as before. "You're wasting time standing out here while she could be inside already being seen to." With every sharp word coming out of Tiran's mouth, Lara flinches in Selon's arms. He turns his body partially away from Tiran as if he can shield her from the male's severe tone.

"You're not helping," Selon says in a soft voice. He wants to rage at Tiran but worries that anything but gentle words might send Lara into a horrible downward spiral. So far, she's holding herself together, just barely. She's upset and exhausted, but she isn't struggling against him or running away in a blind panic or gasping because her fear won't let her take a deep breath.

"She doesn't feel safe in your house, Tiran," he explains. "She doesn't want to go back in there."

Tiran's impatient sound makes Lara's entire body jerk. "Don't be mad," she breathes out. "Please, no one be mad."

"You're not helping," Mara hisses at Tiran.

"What else can I do here?" Tiran rages at his mate. "She needs to be taken indoors and looked after!"

Instead of telling him to quiet down, Mara kicks him in the belly with enough force to make him stagger. The sounds of Tiran's aggravation and Mara starting a physical altercation make Lara jerk and twitch in his arms.

Frantic to take her someplace where she can recover, he turns and starts walking away. The men with him don't comment, only throw disgusted looks over at Tiran, who has yet to quiet down, even after the blow from Mara.

He's only gone a few steps when Deena grabs his arm and turns him in another direction.

"The shuttle," Deena tells him firmly. "The only place she's going to feel safe right now is in that shuttle." She regards the guards. "Trust me, I know what I'm talking about. Let Selon take her. She feels safe with him. I've never seen her wake up from an adrenaline overload this scared without having a full panic attack."

Selon kisses Lara gently on the crown of her head. "Do you want to be in the shuttle? Would that make you feel better?"

"Shuttle," she agrees without bringing her head up, shivers racking her body. "No house. Shuttle."

"I don't think—" Tiran growls out from behind them, but Deena cuts him off harshly, her earlier vulnerability gone now.

"You don't get a say in this," she retorts harshly as she tugs Selon along. "You didn't keep her safe. You brought us here. Forced us here, actually, but you didn't keep her safe." Selon looks over his shoulder to see Tiran blanch, his blue scale pattern going pale at the accusations. It's telling that he doesn't try and defend himself. Half his bluster and rage no doubt stem from his feelings of inadequacy.

"Selon," he calls out, making Selon stop and turn. Giving him a harsh look, Tiran's tone is full of disapproval. "Fine, the shuttle then," he bites out, his sharp, clipped words making Lara whimper. "But don't you dare take advantage of this situation. I see how you are with her right now. I'll be bringing this up to your superiors."

"Do as you see fit," Selon says with a glare, but keeps his voice gentle.

"And I will—" he starts to say, but Mara hauls off and punches him, knocking him back a step and bloodying his nose. Tiran looks stunned as Mara points to the house. "You, inside," she snarls, then turns to Sarin and Titin. "You two get Selon and Lara to the repair bay and into a shuttle. Guard the damn bay and call in reinforcements." She looks at Deena who's sneering back at her. "And you can do whatever the hell you like."

Mara turns to Selon, her face full of concern and worry. "You, please help her."

Selon nods and turns, walking in the direction of the port with Deena leading the way. Sarin and Titin fall in step with him, both of them talking into their communicators, making sure the path is clear and more guards are posted. Selon has never been so happy to see the port in his life. With a feeling of relief, Sarin and Titin escort him into the bay and then to the shuttle. When the shuttle hatch seals behind them, he feels Lara relax slightly.

The seats are still in the bed configuration, so he strides over and sits, holding her gently in his lap and whispering words in her ear. He tells her she's safe, that he's proud of her, that he won't ever let go of her. Slowly her legs relax, and her arms fall from around his neck. She huddles down, drawing her arms between them and tucking her head against his chest.

She's still cold, so he reaches for one of the blankets and wraps it around her. It's not long before she's warming up, and her body is starting to slump sideways. She's falling asleep again, both her mind and body pushed beyond reasonable limits.

She fights it though, trying in vain to keep herself upright against him.

"Sleep, sweet *shamira*," he whispers to her. "I'm here."

Weakly, she nods her head once. Selon carefully lays them down on the bed, making sure she's on top of him and keeps his hands loosely around her. She gives a soft sigh, and Selon feels her relax into him, giving up the fight and letting unconsciousness take over.

"I'll always be here," he promises her sleeping form.

CHAPTER

18

Lara comes awake slowly, keeping her body still and trying to figure out why she hurts. She can tell she's lying on Selon, and she gives a little sigh of contentment. His warm body feels good against hers, and his comforting scent fills her nose. She can tell by his even breathing that he's still asleep. She doesn't want to wake him, but she desperately needs to stretch her stiff and sore muscles.

She starts to move one leg, straightening it until a cramp tightens painfully in her calf. She gives a little gasp of pain, and Selon wakes up under her, sitting up and hugging her tightly to his chest.

"What's wrong?" he demands, running his hands up and down her back. "Tell me where it hurts. Don't be afraid."

Startled, Lara tries to get off his lap to stretch the cramping muscle, and he loosens his arms to allow her to move. "Calf," she grits out, and Selon looks over and sees the knotted muscle. He moves quickly, gently setting her aside and kneeling at her feet, his large hands kneading and stretching the tightened muscle. The air whooshes out of Lara's lungs as the muscle starts to relax. That was a bad one. She smiles down at Selon gratefully, then her brows furrow in puzzlement.

"Why are you dressed?" she asks, then looks down at herself to find she's naked but filthy. She brings up her hands to find broken, jagged fingernails; then she notices her wrists. They're bruised with marks that look like they were made by tight binding. "What happened?" she whispers, unable to stop examining her abused wrists.

"You don't remember?" Selon asks quietly, now just stroking his hands up and down her leg. She looks over at him. He looks so concerned she wants to soothe him.

"I remember visiting you," she starts, then looks around. "We were at your house, and now we're in the shuttle." She closes her eyes and concentrates. "I was at your house. I needed to go back to Tiran's house. We didn't want anyone to worry if they found me missing the next morning. We walked back, and I watched you leave." She smiles a little. "I love watching you walk. You're so handsome." She frowns. "I was happy and . . ." Her eyes fly open to meet his. "There was a man. He took me."

"We tracked you to his house," Selon tells her. "But you had already escaped."

"He was going to rape me," she whimpers. "I couldn't make him stop. I couldn't do anything. He bound my arms and legs . . . he touched me." She hunches into herself, crying out as the memories flood back. Selon holds her tight against him, cooing words of comfort to her as she sobs. He rocks her slowly while she cries. She has no idea how much time passes. It doesn't matter. She cries out all the terror and helplessness she went through. Selon's hold doesn't waver.

Finally, when the tears are finished and her mind feels empty, she sits up. She rubs dirty hands over her gritty, red eyes, and wrinkles her nose in distaste.

"I want to shower," she tells him in a watery voice.

"Considering where I found you, I'm not surprised," he murmurs. "I want to go into the cleaning unit with you, but it's very small here on the shuttle. Do you think you can handle being in a small space with me?"

She thinks about it, pictures sharing such an enclosed place with someone as large as Selon. The idea of it doesn't cause any panic or fear. All she can think of is how comforting his presence near her will be.

"Please come in with me," she agrees. "Help me clean his memory off my skin and then hold me again."

"It would be my fondest wish," he responds and helps her stand. Her legs feel a little shaky and the bottom of her feet hurt.

The pain makes her wince, but it's not enough to keep her from bathing.

"Your feet are torn up from running in the jungle barefoot. I'd like to carry you, if you'll let me." The request is soft, gentle, and Lara doesn't even need to think about it. She nods her head and turns slightly to make it easier to lift her. He cradles her to his chest and nuzzles her hair. "I promise I won't do anything you find uncomfortable. I won't scare you."

"You could never scare me," she assures him. She can't imagine Selon doing anything to cause her fear. Even when she saw nothing but need and lust in his face, he was only gentle with her.

He maneuvers the two of them into the cleaning unit and activates it with his voice. He sets her down and starts to wash her as best he can with the few supplies available. Lara remains still, enjoying his touch and slow movements. It's not until he picks her up again that she realizes he's still fully clothed.

"You're soaked," she murmurs tugging at his shirt.

"That will happen when you step into a cleansing unit with your clothes on." He lowers her to the bed.

"You need to take these off," she demands and tugs the shirt a little more forcefully.

He pulls her hand away from his shirt and gives it a small kiss before letting go. "I didn't want to cause you any distress by stripping. I don't have any other clothes to change into. This outfit will dry out. I'll be fine."

"No, you must be uncomfortable. Just take them off and go naked."

"Remember the part where I'm trying not to cause you any fear?" he reminds her.

"I've seen you naked before," she points out. "I like you naked. When you're naked your skin feels very good against mine."

"But I," he starts, then takes a deep quivering breath. "I don't have the best control over my body right now."

"Because your male part is full of blood?" she asks, eyeing the front of his pants. "I know it's large, but I'm not worried. You haven't accidentally knocked me out with it yet." She meant to tease him, to show him she isn't fearful of him. But instead of laughing, he bends his head away from her.

She reaches out and draws his face back to her, surprised to see dread in his eyes.

"I wouldn't survive," he tells her in a voice hoarse with

emotion. "I wouldn't survive if you looked at me with fear. If you saw him instead of me."

She places her hand on his crotch, feeling his length, and he hisses with need at her touch. "I could never fear you," she assures him. "There is no other male I could let touch me but you. There is no other male who could make me feel this way." She takes her hand off his erection and draws his face close to hers. The scales on his head are vacillating between dark blue and purple.

"When I was taken, when he ripped my clothes off and told me he would force me, all I could think of was you. When he washed your scent off me, I made myself picture you in my mind. I heard you telling me to breathe. Your voice telling me I'm stronger than I think. I could've panicked. I could've shut down and let the man do as he wished. I could have shut my eyes and just waited for it to be over. But instead, I thought about escape."

"You did escape," Selon affirms. "My sweet *shamira*, you saved yourself."

"Only because I had you in my head to keep calm. Your voice to keep the panic at bay. How could I ever be afraid of you when you're the reason I feel safe?"

Selon makes a small sound in the back of his throat, and Lara knows it is from distress. She pushes herself off the bed and onto him, knocking him backward on the floor. She gasps a little at the feel of his cold, wet clothing against her skin, but refuses to let go. He doesn't struggle under her, but his body is stiff and tense.

"I can't imagine my life without you," she tells him. "I can't imagine trying to be brave without you. I don't even want to try."

"Let me up," he begs. Feeling rejected, she moves away from him, only to watch with satisfaction as he strips himself, tossing the wet clothes aside. "Bed," he orders and points, so she moves out of the way so he can lie down, his fierce cock pointing at the ceiling.

"I think I'd like to climb a mountain today," she tells him, and he looks confused as she climbs on top of his warm, inviting body. He goes to close his arms around her, but she doesn't lie on top of him. Instead, she takes his erection in one hand and strokes it.

"Oh, sweet *shamira*," he whispers. "I can just hold you. We don't need to do this now. My affection isn't contingent on us sharing pleasure."

"But maybe I want to," she challenges him, letting her

drying hair fall into her face. Looking through the black mass made the declaration easier to voice. "Maybe I want to feel you inside of me. Feel you touch me. Feel you all around me."

"Can I kiss you first?" he asks, sitting up so he can bring his lips to hers. "Can I put my mouth on you first? I feel like I'm a man dying of thirst, and you're the only thing that can save me."

His words make her flush with need, and she feels herself dampen his skin where her sex is resting. She can tell he smells it because his nostrils flare. He tips her backward until she's the one laying on her back. Then he moves his head between her legs, kissing the insides of her thighs. He scrapes his canines along her skin, making her moan a little. He makes his way to her sex so slowly she wraps her legs around his chest, trying to use her heels to drag his mouth closer.

"Stop that," he orders her. "Your feet are hurt, and you might damage yourself further."

"I'll damage you," she retorts breathlessly and tugs helplessly at him. She feels him smile against the skin of her leg. "I know you're teasing me on purpose. Please do that thing with your mouth again. Please!"

"For someone who claims to be timid and fearful, you're awfully demanding," he observes and nips her. She gasps and wiggles. He reaches up her body with one hand, cupping a breast and thumbing the nipple, making her moan again. She looks down at his face, full of lust and want without a hint of trepidation. She loves that face and the man it belongs to.

She opens her mouth to tell him she loves him when he finally puts his mouth right on her clit and starts to suck. She gives a startled scream and moves her hips against him. She slams her thighs together from the intensity, but his shoulders keep her from boxing him in the head.

His one hand never stops caressing her breast, and the other is at her vagina, fingers gently probing. He slips one finger in, making her jolt from the pleasurable sensation. He strokes the finger inside of her, making her body tense and bow.

Between his mouth lavishing her with attention and his fingers working inside her, it's not long before she's cresting a wave of pleasure. A little scream escapes her as the orgasm consumes her, but he doesn't stop. He keeps going until she can't stand it any longer. "Please," she pants. "No more."

He eases away from her and crawls up next to her on the bed, stroking his hand down her body, from collar bone to thigh. She can feel his hard cock pressing into her side, but when she moves to touch it, he pulls her hand away and lays it on her belly.

"Not right now," he tells her softly. "I need to hold you right now, as much as you'll let me." She reaches her hand up to caress his head.

"Let me get on top," she requests, and he rolls on his back without a word.

Coordinating her body is a little harder than she expects, but she manages to flop herself onto him. She's not sure, but he might have stifled a laugh when he put a helping hand on her ass.

Once on top of him, she snuggles down into her favorite position. His erection is now pressed against her belly, and she rubs against it a little. He gives a little groan but does nothing to stop her.

"You needed to love me," she tells him quietly. "Now I need to love you also."

She wiggles her hips until the head of his cock is resting against her opening, and she slowly lowers her hips. She's so wet he glides into her, making her feel deliciously full. "You feel so good," she moans.

"So do you," he assures her, and she feels his hands grip her thighs. She knows he's fighting to control himself, and she has absolute faith he can.

She lowers herself until he fills her, and her sensitive clit rubs delightfully against him. She meant to move back up his length, draw away from him and slide back down. But she can't seem to keep herself from grinding against him, to push that small bundle of nerves ruthlessly into his firm flesh.

He groans under her, and the sound of his need and enjoyment increases her own. Soon she's pushing even harder against him, unable to draw away from the friction that's rapidly bringing her to another climax.

She knows she's close, and then she feels him growl under her, and his cock releases his seed, filling her with a warmth that causes a chain reaction in her body. Her skin flushes and a second orgasm explodes through her, even more intense than the first. Her back bows, and a small, strangled scream escapes.

Shaking from the sensation overload, she collapses on him, tucking herself against his sweating chest. She can feel him panting under her as she tries to get her breathing under control. When both their hearts finally calm, Selon tries to move out from under her but stops when she grumbles in displeasure.

"I need to see to your feet and wrists," he tells her.

"No," she responds. "You need to stay and cuddle me, and

we need to take a nap. My wounds will heal fine. I'm tough."

"Of that I have no doubt," he assures her. "But I'm worried about infection."

"Stay," she orders. "I won't get sick. I promise."

"We can remain like this for a little longer," Selon compromises. "But then I'll look after you, agreed?"

"You already did," she says, looking up to give him a cheeky grin. Instead of returning her grin, his expression turns solemn.

"You're the most beautiful thing I've ever experienced," he tells her, and she feels her heart swell with emotion.

"I'm glad you think so," she answers. "Because I'm never letting go."

CHAPTER

19

Selon winces as he watches Lara bang the edge of a thruster mount with a massive hammer. The mount is reluctant to bend, but after half a dozen blows it finally gives. "Does no one read schematics," she grumbles darkly to herself as she leans in close to examine the reshaped edge. "I told them I needed an A fitting, but no, they send me a C fitting. I know they look a lot alike, but now the edge will trail and cause wake when the ship hits the atmosphere. Idiots. Even after doing this, there will still be an atmospheric wake. I should just cut it off." She keeps mumbling to herself, and Selon smiles with affection at her typical work-focused-Lara-rambling.

Knowing better than to ask her any questions while she's this focused, he turns his attention to his data pad and the report he's been reading. Nonin, the man who kidnapped Lara, is now being held on the smaller of Hissa's two moons, Diminish. He's being treated and medicated, but Selon wonders how many more men are far more fragile than the Council realizes. How many men might do what Nonin did because they're on the very edge of sanity?

Selon knows Nonin is sick and needs healing, but if the man had succeeded in raping Lara, there's no way Selon could have kept himself from murder. Even now, he fights the urge to find the male and pummel him. The torment he put Lara through is inexcusable, and ever since that night, Selon refuses to leave her side, fearful that if she's out of his sight for even a moment, she'll be taken from him again.

Of course, keeping her in sight is easy when she won't even talk about leaving the hangar. In the five days since the kidnapping, Lara has refused to take one step out of the repair bay and will only sleep in the shuttle. Meals, clothes, and other supplies arrive several times a day, and thousands of letters flood in begging Lara to forgive Hissa for her experience.

He didn't mind staying in the big bay with her for the first few days, but he's starting to miss fresh air and wishes he could go for a run. He hopes he can convince her to maybe climb the tower tonight, watch shuttles land, and stargaze. It would be a welcome diversion for them both, and a stepping-stone to getting her out of the hangar on a regular basis.

"Hello?" a voice calls out from the front of the bay, and Selon looks up to see Deena walking in.

Lara gives a sound of delight and sprints across the bay. When she gets to Deena, she picks up the smaller woman and swings her around, ignoring the pilot's sounds of annoyance. When she stops swinging Deena, she doesn't let go but holds her in a fierce hug.

"You're like a rabid Mirani!" Deena grumbles but hugs Lara back.

"You always say that," Lara retorts, finally letting go of her dearest friend. Once her feet are on the ground, Deena takes half a step back with an indulgent smile but wary eyes.

"I say it because it's true," Deena says with a little laugh.

"But you always let me hug you as long as I want." Lara pokes Deena in the side. "Admit it, you enjoy it."

"If I do, I'm never admitting it," Deena says with her familiar half grin as she eyes Lara critically. "You look rested and recovered," she says with approval.

"I'm feeling much better," Lara admits and shyly glances over at Selon and then back at Deena.

"Well, I have a couple of messages to give you," Deena tells them but doesn't pull out a data pad or any memory paper.

"Messages from who?" Lara asks, her expression turning cautious. She talks to Mara on the large display every day but refuses to interact with Tiran. When he appeared on the display after the first day in the bay, she ducked her head and turned away. When he called for her to please speak to him, she walked into the shuttle until the connection was terminated. She also won't read the letters he's sent. His harsh words while she was at her most vulnerable cut deep, and Selon knows she is much more likely to evade Tiran for the rest of her life rather than face him.

"First thing, Tiran is sorry and wishes to make a formal apology, which includes swords," Deena tells her with a grin. "If you agree, then he gives you a sword, and you can cut him up with it. I'll do it for you if you're interested. Heck, I'll do it even if you aren't interested. That guy's seriously getting on my nerves. A little blood loss might make him more tolerable."

Lara gives her a strained smile. "I'm not interested in making anyone bleed. I only want to be heard. Tiran doesn't want to listen."

Deena shrugs. "You're not wrong. He only seems to listen to Mara, and even then, she has to punch him in the face sometimes." If Selon didn't know better, he'd think Deena was exaggerating. But he has witnessed firsthand how Mara is forced to extremes to gain Tiran's attention. It's one of the reasons Lara won't even talk to him over a communicator. His inability to soften his voice or notice what it does to her has made him persona non grata for her.

This conversation is making Lara tense, so he places himself close behind her. He's not touching her, but as always, she knows exactly where he is without needing to look. With a soft sound, she leans back and grabs one of his hands to clutch to her chest, hugging his arm like a child might hug a favorite soft toy.

Lara pointedly glances over at the thruster mount she was just pounding on. "I still have a lot to get done today. What are the other messages?"

"Right, you want to get back to work. Well, all of Hissa got together to give you a gift," she tells her with real excitement. "I'm here to take you to it."

Stiffening, Lara holds onto his arm even tighter. "I'm not leaving here," Lara tells her flatly. "I'm not going out."

Deena doesn't seem phased by Lara's refusal. "Just peek out the door. You can see it from there."

Now Lara's interest is piqued. "Is it a shuttle?"

"Something like that," Deena grins even wider and takes a step back. "Come on, Lara, I know you better than anyone, except maybe Selon over there. That means you need to trust me when I tell you, you're going to love this!" Deena's almost dancing with excitement, and Selon finds his curiosity on the rise. Deena rarely gets excited like this and never uses more body movement than necessary. He's never seen her act this way before.

"I don't know," Lara hedges, eyeing the door to the bay suspiciously. Both he and Deena remain silent as Lara stares at the door, waging an internal debate about leaving.

"Fine, you can show me," she says, coming to a decision. She stops clutching his arm to her chest but keeps her fingers twined in his. With a deep breath, she follows Deena. Selon walks next to her, happy to have her holding his hand. When they reach the door, Deena grabs it, but instead of just flinging it open, she gives Lara a little wink. "I'll only open it a crack so you can see."

Lara nods, and he watches her prepare to face the dangers of the world outside the repair bay. She pulls the tie out of her hair, so it hangs in her face, squares her shoulders, and tightens her hand in his. Deena pushes the door open just a little and urges Lara to lean forward. Selon doesn't want to crowd her so has no idea what she sees that makes her gasp. He's in shock when she pushes past Deena to fling open the door and tug him along behind her as she rushes out.

"It's your new home!" Deena shouts and races after them. The two guards stationed at the door chuckle and fall in step behind the now sprinting Lara.

Selon isn't sure what he's looking at; then it dawns on him what everyone must have done to create Lara's new "home."

Sitting on top of a high system of struts and girders is an old shuttle. Even to Selon's untrained eye, it appears the engines were removed, and the nozzles replaced by large, concave windows. There's a ladder running up the center of the supports to the hatch added to the belly of the shuttle, as well as a lift only big enough for one person on the outside of the supports that ends at the original shuttle hatch.

Lara skids to a halt and turns to him, giving him a quick kiss, then drops his hand so she can run a quick circle around the struts and take in the view of her new home from the ground.

When she finishes her lap, she dances in place next to him, an expression of pure delight on her face. The lift is starting its journey down, but Lara is much too impatient, so she grabs the lowest rung of the ladder. Before Selon can utter a word, she's scampering up, faster than even a Hissa could manage.

Unwilling to be left behind, he starts climbing behind her. He watches her disappear into the shuttle and glances over to see

Deena taking the lift up, a huge grin stretching from ear to ear on the pilot's face. He reaches the shuttle and pulls himself up just in time to hear Lara give a little squeal of delight as she rushes past him to look out the shuttle's added windows.

So much was accomplished in such a short time. It's both admirable and breathtaking. The inside of the shuttle has been gutted, and the wall between the control room and the cargo hold is entirely gone. The functional but drab industrial metal floors are now covered in light-colored wood. The gray walls are all painted in vibrant colors and works of art hang in several places. Massive curtains in emerald green and sapphire blue are draped from the ceiling to separate out an area for the bedroom. Several of the curtains are drawn back to reveal an ornate, round bed covered in maroon blankets and pillows.

He can see the walls in the engine room have also been removed and the engine area replaced by a sitting area filled with the large, fluffy pillows the Hissa favor for lounging. The windows that replaced the mounted engines flood the area with sunlight. The windows are so large that with the curtains pulled back, the windows are able to illuminate the entire shuttle.

"This is amazing!" Lara screams as she rushes past him again to admire something else. She can't seem to be still as she practically runs from one end of the shuttle to another, admiring all the details many men must have slaved over to provide. "I love this home. I've never seen anything grander!"

"It's nice," Deena agrees. "And it'll lock down tight. The hatch in the floor is the same grade as a regular hatch so unless someone has a good size bomb or a lot of time and a big plasma torch, no one is getting in here." She draws Lara over to a control panel near the hatch and the lift. "You can shut down the lift from here, and you can retract the ladder. Someone could still climb up the support struts, but if you lock down the hatches, they aren't getting in. Oh, and this is the best part!" Deena crows and points to a small button next to the control panel. "This electrifies the supporting structure, so you can zap anyone who's trying to climb up. I thought of that one myself! They refused to make it powerful enough to kill, but it will make them let go and fall."

Selon watches Lara's eyes fill with tears. "Thank everyone for me," she demands.

"You should thank them," Deena counters. "Just make a vid recording and send it to the Council. Selon can help you. Then they'll distribute it. A lot of Hissa helped make this happen, and I know some of this stuff is out of their personal homes. None of them expect you to meet with them. They only want you to feel safe and cared for."

"I'll make a vid," she agrees quickly, rubbing a few stray tears away. "Can you make a list of all those that worked the most? I want to send them personal notes of thanks."

"Then you need to send one to Tiran," Deena says with deliberate blandness. "Because he's the mastermind behind this."

"Tiran?" Her face is nothing but shock.

"He's the one that took this idea to the Council. He's the one who found the old shuttle and got all the crews organized to retrofit it for you. I know you've been ignoring him, and for good reason, but I think maybe it's time to forgive and forget. He is in a Family Pact with your sister, after all."

"I don't know," Lara says hesitantly.

"You know me," Deena says. "I don't say things to make people happy."

"Of that, no one has doubt," Selon murmurs, making Lara giggle and Deena throw him a wry look.

"Right, so if I'm asking you to give him one more chance, then you know you probably should," Deena continues. "You don't have to forgive him, but maybe hear him out? He's so depressed that even I feel bad for him. And this has been hard on Mara too."

"But I talk to Mara," Lara protests.

"And Mara loves Tiran and you. She feels like she needs to pick one of you, and it's tearing her apart. I might not be Tiran's biggest fan, but I don't hate the guy either. And Mara might be bossy as hell, but she's growing on me."

Lara is silent for a moment, looking over the splendor of her new home. "Tomorrow," she finally tells Deena. "Bring him to me tomorrow."

"Great," Deena says with relief. "The last message I have to give is that one of the Menders at medical is begging to come see you. He wants to check on your health and get some samples for testing."

"Perhaps after Tiran," Lara says with a frown. "Maybe. Let me deal with Tiran first."

"I'll tell them what you said," Deena says with a small frown of her own. "But sooner or later you're going to need to make an appearance, even if it's by a communicator. Everyone's worried. I've had to talk to the Council twice now. Those guys need to learn to listen better. But if you talk to even one of them, I won't get dragged in again."

"I have a feeling all of Hissa needs to learn to listen

better," Selon pronounces grimly.

Deena nods and turns to leave, glancing over at him. He's not sure how to read the look on her face but thinks it might be a combination of worry and sympathy. "Right, I'll be going then. Leave you and Selon to check out the new house." Before she can make it back out to the lift, Lara grabs her in a last hug and Deena's expression is pure exasperation. "What is it with you and all the hugging?" she demands, and Lara giggles.

"You love it," she retorts, and Deena gives an exaggerated sigh, pulling Lara off her.

"I'll never admit it," she calls back and slips out the hatch. It shuts behind her with a soft hiss, and Lara rushes off again to continue her exploration. Selon meanders after her, touching the soft fabrics on the bed, running his hands down the smooth painted walls, and opening a food storage container to find it brimming with delectable items.

Suddenly, she is at his side, hugging him with enough strength to make the air in his lungs whoosh out. "This is mine!" she declares with a delighted laugh. Her tone and body movements remind him of the first night they spent in the shuttle after the port was mobbed by miners.

Her jubilation at her new home is infectious. "Yes, all yours."

"Come look!" she grabs his arm and drags him along. "They expanded the cleaning unit. It's huge now." He dutifully admires the larger cleaning unit, happy to note it could now easily accommodate them both.

A soft trilling sound echoes through the space, and the two of them glance around, confused. After a few moments it sounds again, and Selon notices a panel near the hatch is lit up.

That makes him hazard a guess. "I think that is to make you aware of guests." He walks over to the panel and taps it. Tiran's face appears. He can tell by the background he's standing at the bottom of the lift and decided to arrive ahead of schedule. It's something he should have excepted from the impatient male.

"Stay," he orders Tiran and then ends the communication.

Unable to see who he's talking to; Lara gives him a curious look as he walks to her. He tries to think of the best words to use. "Tiran is outside," he starts, and when her expression darkens, he pauses.

"He can stay outside," she grumbles.

"I'm not happy with him either. He's acted far too overbearing with you. The problem is that he doesn't know how to interact with anyone less fierce than Mara and Deena. His inability to change has driven a wedge between him and Mara. She's been living in my empty house since the day we brought you back and refuses to see Tiran." He thinks about the image he was sent along with the daily report on the human women. Mara looks pale and wan, far from her usual vibrant self.

"She can come live here with me," Lara announces eagerly. "There's plenty of room. We could make another bedroom with some more curtains."

"You know that's not a solution," Selon points out gently, and Lara's shoulders slump. He gives her time to mull over the issue, and she finally gives a reluctant nod.

"Fine, I'll talk to him. Or I guess let him glower at me." She moves to the hatch, and Selon steps in front of her.

"Let me go down first," he insists, and she takes a quick step back.

"Sure," she says quickly, eager for anything to delay the meeting. Selon leans over to give her a quick kiss.

"You are such a brave, beautiful female," he tells her.

"Only because of you," she tells him with wide, honest eyes. "No one else could give me the strength you give me."

"I didn't give," he tells her with a heartfelt smile. "I only revealed what was already there."

Lara's expression goes from resigned to lustful in an eye blink. "I wouldn't mind if you revealed a little more!"

"When this is over, we will come back up and spend the rest of the day, uh, christening, your new home," Selon promises, and Lara gives a throaty laugh.

"Get going," she demands. "The sooner this is over, the sooner we can play."

Without further urging, he opens the hatch and heads down in the lift, finding a scowling, impatient Tiran waiting for him. Selon can see the separation from Mara is taking its toll on him as well. He looks like he isn't sleeping, and Selon can smell fear and desperation rolling off him in waves.

"Lara needs to forgive me and tell Mara she's forgiven me," Tiran demands the moment Selon steps off the lift. "Mara won't see me, and the council has given her twenty guards. Twenty males are surrounding her. I can't even smell her when I get close to the house. All I can smell are those men. She won't talk to me. If she would just talk to me!" Tiran's tirade suddenly stops, and he grabs Selon's upper arm with a bruising grip. "I can't exist like this. My heart is missing."

Selon feels bad for Tiran but knows the man brought it on himself. "Lara's willing to come down and talk."

Tiran's grip on his arm loosens, and he looks like he might fall to his knees to thank Selon. "Anything I have is yours," he promises.

"No," Selon tells him quickly, looking up to see the lift is already back at the top ready to collect Lara. "It's not that easy. You need to pay close attention to what I'm about to tell you, because this is your only chance. You need to listen to Lara."

"But I do," Tiran protests. "I always—"

Selon cuts him off with a glare. "No, you don't," he counters. "You talk over her. You order, and you demand, but you don't listen. You expect her to make you listen like Mara does. But Lara isn't Mara. She can't make you listen, so you roll right over her. You put her in the position of a slave."

Those words make Tiran flinch as if Selon hit him. "I would never—" he starts to say, but Selon gives a little growl. The sound of primal anger coming from one so normally reserved and controlled as Selon makes Tiran pause with surprise.

"How did you know she wanted this type of dwelling?" Selon asks, pointing to the ship on stilts.

"Deena told us, and we . . ." Tiran starts to explain, but Selon cuts him off.

"Exactly, Deena told you. Not Lara. Who got Lara a craft to fix and tinker with?"

"You did." Tiran's voice is so soft it's almost a whisper, his entire body stiff with realization. "Why didn't she tell me?"

"She tried, but you don't know how to listen." Selon looks up. Lara is almost in earshot. "Don't interrupt her. Don't speak right after her. Give yourself time to understand what she is telling you. You can't only listen to her words. Pay attention to what she tells you with her smell and body language."

"I'm not as skilled as you about these things," Tiran admits, fear covering his face.

"You don't need to be," Selon assures him. "Everything Lara feels is on display. She has no ability to hide her emotions." Tiran only has time to nod at Selon's words before Lara is there, stepping off the lift and moving close to Selon for comfort.

She picks up one of his hands and holds it in both of hers. She must have taken the tie out of her hair on the way down in the lift because now it's loose and covering part of her face so she's looking at Tiran through thick, shiny, black locks. Her body is tense next to him, and he gives her hand a little squeeze of reassurance.

Tiran takes a step back to give them a little space and clears his throat. He opens his mouth to speak but then closes it again. Selon can tell he's struggling to keep himself from breaking down and begging Lara to forgive him. Or maybe demanding she talk Mara into accepting him back. He's struggling with words. Struggling to ignore his instincts to force everything into place. Force isn't going to work here. Tiran's going to need to learn finesse.

"I examined the shuttle you are working on," he tells her. She gives a little start of surprise at his words. Her reaction to his words makes it apparent that this isn't what she expected from Tiran. "You're a very skilled engineer."

"I'm not an engineer. I'm a mechanic," she responds, her voice so quiet it's almost a whisper.

Tiran shakes his head slightly. "I think you have the mind of an engineer. Would you be interested in taking some classes? After you started working on the booster assembly, I interviewed some of the pilots. It took a while, but they finally started confessing how difficult flying the overloaded shuttles can be. Only the pilots knew about the issue and never said anything, but you noticed."

Selon can feel some of the tension in Lara's body ease.

"I'm not sure about taking classes." Her voice is a little stronger now. "But I would like to keep working on the shuttles and maybe other craft. I'd like to see the mining operation on one of the moons too."

Selon watches Tiran fight his initial reaction: adamant rejection. Tiran's suggestion of taking classes is only a ploy to get her away from the skilled labor she enjoys so much. Selon feels disappointment and knows it shows on his face when Tiran glances over and his blue scale pattern flashes brown with frustration.

"You like to fix craft?" he asks quickly, turning his attention back to Lara. "Can you tell me why you enjoy it so much? I'd like to understand."

Selon also glances down at Lara and watches her struggle with the need to be heard and understood and the equally powerful wish to be ignored and overlooked. He watches her take a few deep breaths as she drops her eyes to the ground and starts to talk.

"Engines are complicated, but they make sense," she tries to explain. "The rest of the world doesn't make any sense to me. There's pain and misery, and some people will hurt you because it gives them pleasure. To them, your pain doesn't matter at all. But engines would never do that. When I work on them, I'm making them better, healing them, protecting them. They run well under my care. When I heard Deena laugh because Ally worked better for her, it made me feel needed and accomplished. Do you understand?"

Tiran silently regards her for a moment, his expression blank. Selon tries to figure out what the man's thinking, until he realizes Tiran's waiting for Lara. When she risks looking up at him, he gives her an approving smile. It's a level of patience Selon's never seen Tiran display.

"I think I finally do understand. One of my main duties for Hissa is programming. I integrate systems on ships and on the mining colonies. I was sent to Bicoma because I'm the best we have, and we hoped to barter my skills for help. I might complain, but I do enjoy pulling panels apart and trying to figure out why components aren't working as they should." Tiran stops to take a few deep breaths of his own and then continues. "I would feel less than whole if I wasn't allowed to do these things. If I wasn't allowed to exercise my skills. I can only imagine the torture it must have been in the last months to be denied something that brings you not only satisfaction, but pleasure as well."

"Yes," Lara nods her head happily. "That's exactly it. I'm very thankful the Hissa saved me and Deena. And then Selon entered my life, and everything got better. But I want to work on the shuttles too. If I can help at the mines, I'd like to do that as well."

Tiran gives a thoughtful nod. "That can be arranged, but first we need you to help us with our shuttles. It'll take a while. There are over two hundred in use right now, and almost that many sitting on the discard field for want of repairs. I wondered why we seemed to go through shuttles so fast, but the mining on the moons makes us so rich we kept buying shuttles instead of bothering to figure out why they were breaking so quickly."

"Hundreds?" Lara squeaks out, but her face isn't worried; it's full of anticipation.

"We might need to move you into a different bay," he says, thinking out loud. "Maybe you could consider teaching some of our men how to help. It would be nice to get the fleet running efficiently now that we are aware of the problem."

Selon worries Tiran might be a little too enthusiastic in his new approach to Lara, but when he looks down at her, he sees nothing but excitement on her face.

She looks up to meet Selon's gaze, giving her head a shake

so her hair falls away to reveal her grinning face. "I guess I should go talk to Mara."

"Not yet," Tiran says, drawing their attention and surprise. "I'm not done yet." He drops to his knees in front of Lara, locks his hands behind his back, and bows his head.

"I need to offer you a formal apology and beg your forgiveness," he tells her. "I've been a bully to you. I never listened and you suffered because of my negligence. I have no right to your mercy, no expectation of kindness or compassion. You must do as you see fit, but I tell you with all the truth in my heart, if you deign to forgive me, I'll endeavor to rectify my behavior and treat you as the skilled and strong female you are." The formal words, spoken with deep sincerity, touch Selon's heart, and he can't imagine sweet, kind Lara being able to refuse.

His suspicions are confirmed when he hears a sniff and watches with pride bursting in his chest as Lara reaches over and places a hand on Tiran's shoulder.

"Please get up, brother," she whispers. "There's nothing to forgive." Stumbling to his feet, Tiran wraps his arms tightly around his chest and Selon suspects he's doing it to keep himself from snatching Lara up in a grateful hug.

"You are a kind sister," Tiran tells her.

"Let's go talk to Mara," she urges. "The sooner you two are settled, the sooner I can return to working on my shuttle and the sooner Deena can fly it."

"We can only hope that improves her mood," Tiran grumbles.

"Deena or Mara?" Selon asks, and Tiran grunts with displeasure.

"Both," he tells them with a sour expression, making Lara laugh.

Tiran brought a personal transport and hurries them all inside. Soon they're at Selon's small home, and Lara's shocked to see so many guards posted. Every single one of them is armed to the teeth and looking daggers at Tiran as the three of them make their way up the narrow walkway.

"You aren't allowed here," one says, stepping in front of Tiran and stopping their progress. "Lara and Selon may enter, but you're not allowed entrance. The Council decreed it after Mara demanded you be kept away from her."

Tiran is about to open his mouth to protest when a shriek of rage turns all their attention to the front door. Mara stands there, looking a little too thin and pale, staring at the three of them with shock and anger.

"Did you force her here?" she demands, rushing down the path and pulling Lara away from Selon to hug her. "I'm so sorry, Lara. We'll get on Witch and leave. I won't let them hurt you. I'll keep you safe." Mara glares at Tiran. "Haven't you done enough already?"

Lara struggles out of Mara's hold. "Mara, I need to breathe." She gives an exaggerated wheeze and Mara loosens her grip and pulls back.

"He didn't make me come here. I'm here of my own free will," she insists when she can see her sister's face. It's obvious by Mara's expression she doesn't believe Lara's words. "It's true. He made amends," Lara assures her. "He listened to me. Really listened."

Mara looks over at Tiran suspiciously. "Prove it."

Tiran looks helplessly over at Lara, and she shrugs. His eyes fall back on Mara, longing and need radiate off him.

"She fixes ships," he starts hesitantly, and Mara gives a snort of derision.

"We all know that." She squares off with him, her fists clenched. "All of Hissa knows that."

"But she feels about her engines and ships as you feel about your ship, Witch. These machines aren't alive like your Witch, but to her that almost makes them better. A ship won't hit her, torment her, or neglect her. They reward her efforts by running well. And her skills are the way she expresses love to those around her. If she can't repair or tinker, she can't show us how much she cares. Our food storage cabinet always ran too hot at the top and too cold at the bottom. She fixed it the first day she was here. And when the automatic feeders broke on Penon's aviary and his Dovi birds refused to eat out of anything else, she swallowed her fear and asked to be taken over there. She didn't even know Penon yet; he was a friend of mine, not hers. Those actions were her way of telling us she loves us."

Selon knows his jaw has dropped from surprise and looking over at Mara, Lara, and several of the guards, he finds they're all wearing the same expression.

Not only is Tiran not known for his eloquent speech, but some even tease him that the only thing he likes to talk to are computers. And yet, here he is not only explaining how Lara views the world, but also doing it in terms of labor and love.

Tiran has learned to listen to the poetic language that his heart whispers to him since meeting Mara.

With tears in her eyes, Mara launches herself at Tiran, who catches her easily. They hug each other tightly, whispering frantically to each other. When Tiran starts walking the both of them back to his house, none of the guards try to stop them.

"I'm glad that's over," one of them mutters. "She cried all the time. It was breaking my heart."

"It wasn't too much fun when he was roaring at us either," another guard points out. "He might be short, but I know for a fact that man trains with the warriors at the Citadel often. He might be smaller than most, but he's so fast it equals out."

"Only a Hissa would call someone six and a half feet tall short," Lara murmurs to herself with a small grin. She turns to look at Selon, her eyes a little wet with happiness for Tiran and Mara. "Let's head back to the repair bay. I'm almost done, and I want to see the shuttle fly."

"Of course," Selon responds. It only takes a quick look to have half the guards leave their post at the front of the house and fall into position around Lara and Selon. As a unit, they all trek back to the port.

I'm going to need to set up an office in the repair bay, he thinks. *Because I don't plan on leaving Lara any time soon and I don't think she ever plans on being anywhere else but the bay and home.*

As they reach the shuttle bay, one of the guards walking next to Lara pauses, stopping the entire group's progress. He bends over to get a closer look at Lara. Surprised by the move, she ducks back, putting herself mostly behind Selon.

"I'm sorry, Lara Stray," the guard says quickly, straightening up. "I thought I saw something on your neck. I must have been mistaken." To Selon's shock, the guard's scale pattern flashes brown for a brief moment. The man's actions and the flash of brown puzzles and irritates Selon.

"I believe we've arrived," Selon tells the guard with a scowl as he ushers Lara into the bay. He can't believe the guard so casually invaded Lara's personal space, despite the many warnings and decrees issued by the Council. He thinks to send another report out to the Council while Lara works. Maybe he should start interviewing and vetting any of the Hissa that could be assigned to her as a guard.

Lara goes to work as he searches for his data pad, finally finding it under a set of unpacked seals Lara ended up not needing to use. He finds a message on his data pad requesting his immediate attendance at a Council meeting currently in session.

Perfect, he thinks, *I can go over there to make sure they understand how important it is that males don't casually try and interact with Lara.*

He doesn't know either of the guards at the door, so he requests Woken and Sarin, two guards he and Lara both know. When they arrive, he walks up to Lara, who's so immersed in her task that she doesn't realize he's standing over her until he touches her.

"I need to attend a Council meeting," he explains, and his words make her frown. "That guard that got so close to you on the way here is gone. Woken and Sarin will guard you until the second moon rises or you retreat to your shuttle home."

"You won't be gone long, will you? I'll be finished here soon, and I thought we would, uh, explore the new house together. Remember?"

Selon feels his scales flush purple as he swoops down to kiss her. "I look forward to it. I promise to return as swiftly as possible."

"That's fine then," she says, already turning back to her task. "I'll see you soon."

He gives her one last caress and strides out of the bay, determined to be quick with the Council.

As he walks the short distance to the Council building, he laments the lack of Lara's scent in the air. It's almost as if when he's away from Lara the air becomes thin, and colors lose their luster.

And now he's a poet, he thinks ruefully as he makes his way to the Council chambers. Soon all the Hissa men will be like Tiran and himself, besotted and romantic.

He can only hope.

There is a knock at the bay door and Lara looks up to see Woken poking his large head inside. "Lara Stray? May I come in? I won't get too close, but I have very important things to tell you."

He's so massive that Lara's amazed he gets around as well as he does. He might not bump his head on the top of door frames or break chairs when he sits down, but it's obvious that many of his personal items needed to be custom made for his big body. Especially those hands. She watched him sketch once and idly picked up one of his styluses. It was bigger than several of her fingers put together and yet looked petite in his hand.

But for all his size, Woken has a gentle heart. It comes out in his sketches and the way he's so careful around her. Unlike many, he always remembers to keep his voice low, and his movements slow in her presence. Despite his large body, he's rapidly becoming one of her favorite Hissa. He exudes calm almost as well as Selon, even wearing full body armor and carrying weapons like he is now.

"Please come in," she calls back and sets down the tools she gathered to put away. With the craft finished, all that's left is clean up. She walks to meet Woken under the shuttle. His face looks worried, and she feels anxiety uncurl in her belly. "What's wrong, Woken? Has someone been hurt?"

"Nothing like that," Woken assures her, and she notices he's staring at her neck. "You're wearing a high-necked garment today," he comments, and confusion swamps her.

"Yes, and long sleeves and pants. It's to protect me when I have to crawl into tight places," she explains, wondering what this has to do with anything.

"Could you please pull the neck of your shirt down just a little?" He holds out his thumb. "Just this much."

"I'm not injured," she assures him as she hooks a finger at the neck of her shirt and tugs the tough fabric down. There isn't much give so she's only able to reveal her skin to the base of her neck. To show any more she'll need to pull the garment off over her head. "I'd tell you if I was injured."

She watches Woken's eyes widen, and she wonders what he's seeing. Did she hurt herself and not realize it?

She whirls around to one of the landing struts. Its cover makes a good reflective surface. She leans over to look at her neck, gasping when she sees it.

An intricate, red, geometric pattern circles her neck. Snatching a utility knife off a nearby tool bench, she cuts at the fabric so she can pull it down further. The pattern extends out toward her shoulder. "Mating marks," she whispers in shock. "Selon gave me mating marks."

"I didn't believe Luten when he told me you had them," Woken murmurs, eyeing her marks at a respectful distance. "None of us believed you would let Selon get so close to you. We all assumed you would never let any man get close to you. All of your guards saw how much effort it took you to be in the presence of men. But if one was to mate with you, then Selon is the best choice. He's an honorable male, worthy of you. And you've gotten so much better since he's been here."

"I never thought this could happen," Lara admits, realizing she never really thought about a future. She trained herself to always just accept today and wait for tomorrow, never plan beyond the next repair.

Planning a future means she has control of her life, and control is such a foreign concept it terrified her before. But a future with Selon seems feasible. More than feasible, it seems necessary.

There is no future she can imagine that doesn't have him in it.

"Lara, it's important you answer me now." Woken draws her attention back to him. She turns to look at him, letting go of her shirt. "Do you wish Selon to be your male? Do you want him to bear your tattoo and be the father to your young?"

"Children?" To Lara's shock, the idea doesn't cause any panic. Children with Selon would be magical. Who else could possibly nurture and care for a child with her better than Selon?

"Yes, children," Woken repeats, urgency rising in his voice. "Do you want Selon to be yours?"

"Yes," Lara answers without hesitation. "He's already mine." she points to her neck. "I think this proves it."

Woken shakes his head regretfully. "That only means you two can have children together. If you want to keep him, I fear you will need to be very brave."

"What's going on, Woken?" Her heart is beating faster with anxiety. "You're scaring me."

"When Luten saw the marks, he ran straight to the Council. They must have appeared today because someone reviewed yesterday's recordings of you walking, and they didn't show the marks. The marks are clearly visible on the back of your neck now. Selon is standing in front of the Council at this very moment, answering for the crime of bedding you."

"How is that a crime?" Lara's voice is high with shock. "It wasn't rape. I love Selon. I wanted it. He tried to refuse, but I pushed him."

"The Council believes Selon manipulated you. They think he's acted dishonorably and are now passing sentence on him."

She doesn't even need to think about it, she sprints to the door, desperate to save Selon. She almost runs into Deena who must have been on the way to tell her similar information because she doesn't even hesitate when she sees Lara's stricken face.

"This way!" she yells and leads Lara to the Council building at a dead run. Woken and Sarin fall in step behind the two women, yelling at everyone to make way and let the group through.

It takes little time to reach the impressive Council structure, but the massive stone doors bar their entrance. The thirteen-member Council is meant to open and close the heavy doors together as a sign of unity and consensus. Working together, Woken and Sarin manage to pull one of the doors open just far enough to let the two women slide inside.

There is no antechamber; the doors open directly into a

large room where hundreds of Hissa men sit in large wooden chairs. There is a dais at the far end of the room with thirteen men sitting at the top. Lara can see Selon standing in front of the dais, hands bound behind his back and guards on either side of him. By the look of it, the meeting is about to be adjourned.

Lara doesn't have time to pull the tie out of her hair and hide her face. She doesn't have time to let the panic and fear take over. All she can see is Selon, her sweet, wonderful Selon, fresh bruises on his face, with his hands bound behind his back, struggling to pull out of the guard's grip.

"No!" she screams and runs past the seated men who all stare at her in shock. She's thankful no one stands up to stop her. She's not a fighter like Mara. She couldn't beat off any of these men if they stood between her and Selon.

The two guards holding Selon look conflicted as she gets closer. She can tell they don't want to let her get too close to their prisoner, but they also know they shouldn't be too close to her either. She uses that to her advantage and screams again. "Move away from him!"

"My sweet *shamira*," Selon whispers as the two guards move away, allowing Lara to grab him around the waist. "You didn't need to come here. You're so brave. I'll be fine. You can leave," he promises her.

"I'm going to fix this," she says with a last squeeze. It's hard to let go of him, knowing the room is full of men and there's only one way in and out. She's effectively trapped, and she did it to herself.

Determined, she ignores the way her knees feel weak and lets go of Selon to face the Council. Stepping forward boldly, she pulls down the neck of her shirt with shaking hands.

"Selon gave me these marks. He's mine! You can't take him away from me!"

There's a murmur from the crowd, but one of the council members quiets them with a look. "There are things you don't understand about this situation," he tells her with a kind voice.

"We're sorry, Lara Stray, but you might not know all the important facts," another one says. His voice is harsher, and he glowers. For some reason that statement sets the room off into another wave of murmurs, and these sound distinctly angry.

Lara feels her entire body is starting to shake. Adrenaline and fear are coursing through her system. Part of her mind is screaming at her to run and hide from the scowling man looking down at her and all the men whispering in angry voices around her.

The entire room feels too small for the amount of men inside.

Too small for the amount of emotions being displayed.

She looks back at Selon, and he's staring at her with nothing but love and pride. *I'll be strong for Selon because he's been strong for me.*

"I know everything I need to know," she tells the Council in a soft but still clear voice. "Selon is a man of honor and kindness."

"We fear he might have manipulated you," another council member tells her with obvious pity. "You have a fragile mind, little Lara Stray, and he has used this to his advantage. It's our duty to protect you, even from our own men if necessary."

"I pushed him," she insists. "I made him touch me. I wanted it. I demanded it."

"We know you think this," the council member tells her. "But you need to know something very important about Selon. We've learned he kept a secret from you."

Lara looks back at Selon to see he's hanging his head in shame. What could possibly make this wonderful man feel shame? What deep, dark secret could Selon possibly be hiding from her? She thinks back to their first meeting on the tower and all the events that brought them here and understanding dawns.

"Do you think I don't know he is a Mender of the mind? That he works with your most desperate males to ease their mental suffering?" she asks, keeping her eyes on Selon instead of the Council.

His head whips up, face full of surprise. "You knew?"

"I knew," Lara confirms. She points to her head with a small smile. "I'm fearful, not an idiot. They tell me a Mind Mender is showing up to help me with my fear, and then you appear at the door and fulfill all my wishes and make my mind feel better. Of course, I knew you must be the Mind Mender." She ignores the Council as they start to talk quietly among themselves. The room buzzes with conversation, but her entire focus is on the man in front of her.

"You never said anything," Selon murmurs.

Now Lara feels confused. "Why would I need to say anything?"

"Because . . ." Selon starts, then can't seem to finish.

"You thought I'd reject you?" she steps forward and puts her hands on either side of his face, drawing him down until their foreheads touch. "I wanted you to heal me before I even met you. I wanted to be better. I was ready to work on it. I just never expected my healing to be so wonderful. You make me feel safe, happy, and for the first time in my life, you make me enjoy being touched by a male."

"You're so much stronger than any of us realized. And more clever," Selon whispers. She goes on her tiptoes, thinking to kiss him, but a voice from the dais interrupts.

"I see you know much more than we expected, Lara Stray," a council member tells her. "We expected a naïve, broken girl, forever in need of coddling and care. We never expected a woman of courage and skill. We would have done our duty to the first version of you, but we are happy to let this new you claim Selon."

A small cheer erupts from the audience, and she turns away from the Council to wrap her arms around Selon, holding onto him tightly. There's movement out of the corner of her eye, and then Selon's hands are free, and he's embracing her in his unique, gentle hug that only makes her feel warm and comforted and never trapped or scared.

"You saved me," he whispers in her ear.

"You saved me first," she whispers back.

"Hey, if you guys are done with these two, I've got a request," Deena's loud voice makes the room go quiet again. She's standing on one of the wooden chairs back near the door. A disgruntled Hissa male stands close to her, glaring up at the woman who stole his seat.

"What is it you wish to speak with us about, Deena, Captain and pilot of the Ally?" one of the council members asks.

"Deena, formerly Captain and pilot of the Ally," Deena retorts boldly. "The Ally blew up. Now don't think I'm not grateful for the last-minute save, because Lara and I would be dead otherwise. But I'm like Lara. I need a job or I'm going to go crazy."

"What job do you request?" the man standing next to her asks.

"Pilot," she states simply giving him a big smile. "I'm a good one. Let me run shuttles between the moons and the port. Or make deliveries out of the system. I don't care. I just need to fly."

The Council members all lean in together and speak quietly, quickly coming to a decision and turning their attention back to Deena. "We find your request reasonable, but we expect you to go through the same training required of all Hissa pilots."

"But I already know how to fly," Deena whines, and several of the Council members smother laughs.

"Then the training will be easy for you. If you wish to fly, you'll complete the training. Only then will you be issued a ship and a route. This is the Council's final decision."

"Right." Deena shrugs and jumps down from the chair. "Thanks for the loan," she tells the Hissa she stole the chair from and saunters over to Lara and Selon before he can respond.

"So, I guess you're getting a tattoo soon," Deena comments, glancing at Selon's neck; then she turns her eyes to Lara. "I knew you had it in you. You just needed a little time." She winks. "And maybe the right motivation."

Lara gives a little laugh and tightens her hold on Selon.

All thirteen Council members stand up. This must be the cue for everyone else to stand because soon the entire room is on their feet. Then the council member in the very center of the dais speaks loudly to the crowd. "We declare this Council session over. We will open the doors now and bid everyone a good day and bright night. May Brimming bring you love and life and may Diminish keep you safe from strife."

All the men in the room speak in unison, including Selon standing next to her. "Thank you for your service, Council. We give the Moons thanks and hope their bright light will guide you to the best decisions for all of Hissa."

"Thank you for your service, men and women of Hissa. We will endeavor to deserve your trust," the Council replies in unison and steps off the dais. No one else moves as the Council members all make their way to the massive double doors and together push them both open. Lara feels strangely moved by the ceremonial end of the meeting, but also thankful it's all over.

The three of them stay near the dais so everyone else can filter out. No one tries to engage them, respecting the bravery Lara showed and what it must have cost her to speak in front of such a large crowd of males. But many of them eye Deena as they go by. The sour expression on Deena's face makes Lara realize that for all her friend's bravado, she's tired of the unrelenting pressure of Hissa men constantly seeking her out. And, unlike Lara, she doesn't even have a Council decree ordering all the men to keep their distance.

"I'm going to slip out," Deena tells them as the last few men file out. "I don't want to go back to the port with you, and I don't feel like being asked to go home with every guy hanging around outside."

The male whose chair she stole suddenly appears next to them and looks at Deena. He's still scowling. "You should come with me," he tells her.

"Why? Because you have your mother's jewels to give me? Or do you want to dress me in colorful clothes? Or you need to show me some priceless collection or something like that?"

"No, because I'm one of the flight instructors and I can take you to the practice field to start your training," he tells her and looks over at a large window, high in the wall. "We've got just enough time to get one practice in before it's dark. Or were you lying when you said you wanted to be a pilot?"

Deena looks indignant. "I'm already a pilot," she declares.

"Prove it," the man says simply.

"Right!" Deena almost shouts. "Show me the way to the practice field so I can make you feel like an idiot."

"Such a demure, timid female," he states wryly. "It's a wonder no one has won your heart yet." Before Deena can retort, he turns on his heels and strides away, unconcerned whether Deena follows him or not.

"Oh," Lara chuckles as Deena chases after the man. "Deena's going to rip him to shreds."

"No," Selon disagrees as he watches the two leave the building. "Kilan might be the only male who can deal with her."

"Sounds like you know something."

Selon shrugs. "It's not my place to tell his secrets, but I know this male well, and although it would never have occurred to me to match those two, they might be perfect for each other."

Lara jumps up and wraps her arms and legs around Selon. "Just like you and me!" she declares happily.

"Yes," Selon agrees, nuzzling her neck. "Let's go home."

"My home?" Apprehension unfurls inside her. She's not sure Selon will want to live in an old, converted shuttle hoisted high in the air.

"Yes, let's return to our beautiful home," he reassures her, cupping her cheek in his hand and kissing her lips. "I'm afraid you're stuck with me now. Who will save me next time if not you?"

She laughs and hugs him tighter. "Home then," she agrees, letting her head rest on his shoulder as he effortlessly holds her to his chest. "I love you, Selon," she whispers.

"I love you too, my sweet *shamira*," he tells her without breaking stride. Woken and Sarin fall in step behind them as they leave the building, and both guards are grinning from ear to ear.

CHAPTER

21

Lara frowns as she stares at Selon's neck. "There must be something we can put on that to ease the pain."

"There are plenty of things we could do, but we won't. It's important I endure the pain," Selon explains, and Lara gives a huff of discontent. He runs his hand over the fresh tattoo around his throat, a perfect copy of Lara's mating marks. The touch hurts, but the pain only makes him smile with contentment. "My pain and discomfort show my dedication to you. Dulling any of these sensations defeats part of the reason for the tattoos in the first place."

Her frown doesn't go away. "I don't like it."

Selon tugs her into his lap, sighing with pleasure when she settles down with her legs on either side of his hips and her head nestled on his shoulder, her nose pressed against his neck. He can hear her take a deep breath and knows she's pulling his scent into her lungs. The fact that Lara takes such great pleasure in his scent makes him happy, especially when she insists on wearing articles of his clothing when she works, so his smell can comfort her when she's dealing with all the mechanics working with her on the shuttles.

Over the last few months, Lara has blossomed. She manages four repair bays now, and with the help of very conscientious coworkers, she's learning to communicate with the men around her with minimal fear and no panic attacks. It helps that Selon made sure to hand pick each male after extensive interviews and subjected them all to lectures about how best to interact with Lara.

They've all proved to be diligent. Always maintaining distance from Lara, keeping their voices low and even, and even making sure their movements are steady and non-threatening. About four days in, a male hurt himself but was so worried about upsetting Lara, he maintained silence until he could quietly get the attention of another member of the team. Unable to walk, he almost bled to death waiting for someone to get close enough so he could tell them to get help.

Even with that level of dedication to Lara's mental well-being, Selon still hovered protectively for the first few weeks. He only left because Lara kicked him out when he kept stepping between her and the men when they approached her for instructions or to ask questions.

It was with great reluctance that he left, even with her promise to call him when she needed him. So far, she's required his assistance only a few times and none of them were caused by the males working with her. It was always outside factors, a ship crashing on the landing pad, or a miner being so bold as to force his way into her repair bay.

To her credit, after Selon arrived, she calmed quickly and within hours was able to return to work. He might not be happy about that, but he is proud. His Lara has the kind of strength that odes are written about.

Occasionally, Selon misses the early days when Lara wanted only his company, but then he quickly shakes off those thoughts and reminds himself of her amazing transformation. From a woman who panicked at just the sight of a male, to a woman working side by side with dozens of males. This new Lara makes all of Hissa rejoice.

But today there will be no work. Today is the day they formally enter into a Family Pact. Selon received his tattoos, and now a celebration and feast are waiting for them. At the base of their home, tables are laden with food, blankets unfurled and laid out with jewel-toned cushions for guests to recline and eat. Colorful streamers have been strung everywhere, and there's a general air of jubilation among the thousands attending.

Just about all of Hissa wanted to come, but the Council set up a lottery system to keep the numbers limited. Three thousand males won the right to be present at this Family Pact feast, but the rest were not left out in the cold. A remote-piloted, hovering vid capture circles the area, transmitting everything so those who weren't lucky enough to win a spot through the lottery can watch everything.

Around the struts of their home are piles of gifts. When they started amassing earlier the day before, Lara expressed deep displeasure. She didn't want unknown Hissa giving her gifts. It felt wrong because she doesn't even personally know the vast majority of the givers.

To assuage her guilt, she decided she's going to write a personal thank you note to each male who sent a gift. Selon doesn't have the heart to tell her that would only mean more gifts would arrive as soon as word got out that those who sent gifts would receive her attention, even if it's only a few words scribbled on a piece of memory paper.

It doesn't matter. Personal attention from any of the Decanted women has taken on an almost spiritual meaning to Hissa males. Mian, Lara, and Mara might all be in Family Pacts now and unavailable to the single men of Hissa, but they're seen as good luck charms. A word, touch, or note from any of them, especially the still single Deena, is believed to enhance the male potential of finding a Decanted female of his own.

Selon doesn't entirely understand the logic but finds it harmless. And if it helps the men of Hissa cope, then all the better. Hope has been in such short supply for so long that they need all they can get.

"You know everyone is waiting for us?" Selon tells her gently, and she stiffens in his arms.

"I don't want to go down," she whines softly.

"We need to. It'll make all the other men happy to see you. They all dream of finding a Decanted female of their own and the sight of us with matching mating marks will give them hope and help their emotional endurance. It's important or I wouldn't push you."

Lara shakes her head and pouts. "You never push me any further than I can handle. But could we pretend I can't handle this?"

Selon chuckles and gives her a quick kiss before gathering her to his chest and standing up with her secure in his arms. "Enough stalling," he declares and strides over to the lift. "There is merriment waiting for us."

They descend in the small lift together, only able to fit because he holds her so tightly to him. Once on the ground, he sets her on her feet while everyone gathers around them at a respectable distance. There might be thousands in attendance, but every single one of them read the extensive report Selon prepared and agreed to all the rules and conditions of this celebration.

Not only does the crowd stand silent, even after Lara and Selon appear, but the food hasn't been touched yet either. No one's sitting on the soft blankets or relaxing against colorful pillows. No, every single male is standing and watching him and Lara with rapt attention. Eyes bounce from his neck to hers and everyone, even the Council members who are so good at hiding their emotions, display longing.

As Selon and Lara stand on the small stage erected right next to the lift, one of the Council members steps forward. He comes to a stop right in front of them and addresses the crowd.

"I present Selon, first male of the family Hollian, and Lara, one of two twin females of the Decanted Sisters Lost and Stray."

"I wondered how he was going to do that," she mutters in his ear. "You know Mara picked that name because she felt lost without me. I picked Stray because that's what I felt like, an unwanted and abused stray animal. But it doesn't feel right anymore. I don't want to be Lost or Stray."

"What name would you pick to replace Stray?" Selon inquires as the council member drones on about the importance of Family Pacts and the Decanted women to the future of Hissa.

"Probably Star," she tells him. "Because it's always given me peace to watch them from a window as a ship moves. Or maybe Wrench, because it's what I like to do, wrench on things."

"I like Star," Selon murmurs, then looks up and loudly clears his throat. The council member stops talking and turns to the couple with an expectant expression.

"Is there something you would like to add, Selon?" he asks politely.

"I have a thought," he announces. "We are starting a new era, and we will be forming entirely new families with Decanted females. Most of these females probably don't have family names of significance and history. Perhaps we should start a new tradition of the couple deciding on a new family name to pass down to their young."

"I can't take away your family name," Lara says quickly, and Selon quirks his lips.

"Darling *shamira*, I was about to give it up anyway and join the Lost and Stray family. Males on Hissa take the females' family name unless the female indicates otherwise."

"Oh!" Lara says with wide eyes. "I didn't know."

The council member nods with approval. A quick look at his fellow Council members shows their approval as well. "We have no issues with this. What name would you like to put forth as your family name?"

"We wish to be the family Star," Selon requests.

Mara steps forward, Tiran close at her side. "It's a good name," she agrees. "I want to keep Lost because it reminds me that I'm found, but Star suits someone as bright as Lara."

A general sound of approval ripples through the crowd, and the council member turns back to his audience. "I present Lara and Selon, first generation of the family Star." A roar of approval echoes across the port and although Selon can feel her jolt at the sound, Lara doesn't try to duck behind anything or climb him like a tree. He's only mildly disappointed she doesn't need to clamber onto his back because he likes it when she drapes herself over him.

No, she stands there tall and proud as thousands of male voices wash over her. His Lara, who thought herself so broken, just keeps showing how wrong that idea was.

"I can hold you if you're scared," he whispers in her ear, his voice teasing so she knows he's asking because he wants it. Not because he thinks she's going to succumb to panic.

"I'm good right now, but I promise to be very scared later," she whispers back. "When this is all over, I'm going to be so scared you're going to need to distract me."

"How will I be distracting you?" he asks with a husky purr.

"I think it will involve a bed and no clothes," she tells him solemnly and then breaks out into a grin. "And I'm pretty sure it will take all night to comfort me."

"There is nothing I'd like more," Selon promises her, "than to spend the rest of my life seeing to your comfort."

She giggles and nuzzles his neck. "Promise?"

Selon captures her lips with his, kissing them until they are both panting and aroused.

"Promise."

CHAPTER 22

Lara sets the miniature tram onto its track with a huge smile on her face. In the evenings, after work, and after at least one romp in bed with Selon, she's been working on a fun, personal project. Selon doesn't say a word as she carries box after box of random parts home, bits and pieces salvaged from retrofitted shuttles.

From these boxes of castoffs, she's built a miniature track and several trams, keeping them all stored in a cabinet, hidden from Selon until today.

Now, after almost a month of work, she's finally finished and wants to dance with glee. It's not the hardest task she's ever completed, but it's by far the most artistic one. The miniature track runs along the floor against the back wall of the shuttle, then ascends until it's at the height of her head. At the door, she ran the track even higher, putting it almost against the ceiling so it could clear the hatch. After the hatch there's a sharp decline that brings the track down again so it can run under a round window. For the rest of the circuit of the room, the tram runs along the floor.

She hopes Selon likes it because she used some intensely strong epoxy to secure the tram tracks to the wall and she's not sure they're ever coming off. She should have used something that could be removed easily, but the mix she decided on set quickly so she didn't have to stand around for hours holding miniature tram girders in place while the epoxy set.

The effect is so perfect she doesn't even care about the few minor chemical burns on her hands from accidentally getting the mix on herself while she secured everything.

Unlike the real Hissa trams, her toy is powered by the shuttle's electrical system instead of geo thermals, but her miniature version still moves at a slow, lumbering pace, climbing and descending while never speeding up or slowing down.

She built three trams to go on the tracks and set them up at different spots to run the circuit, laughing with delight as they pass by where she's sitting on the floor near the bed.

"Lights, dim to ten percent," she calls out and holds her breath waiting. Gleefully, she sees the tiny lights inside the tram cabins activate. That was the last detail she struggled with before setting up the tracks, getting the toy tram to light up like the real ones do at night.

She hears the hatch to her home open, and she looks over to see Selon step inside. She jumps up and rushes to him, throwing herself into his arms and wrapping her legs around his waist. He's braced for this familiar greeting, so he doesn't stumble, only wraps his arms around her. With a sigh of happiness, he nuzzles her neck.

"You smell good," he murmurs.

"You always say that," she laughs.

"I can't help it if it's always true," he counters and starts walking to the bed.

She starts to wiggle. "Put me down, I have something to show you." He lets her go with obvious reluctance and follows her to the spot on the floor where she sat earlier, surrounded by tools and tiny discarded parts. "Look what I made!" she exclaims, pulling him down to sit on the floor with her.

"What am I looking at?" he asks, peering at the miniature tram track. He follows the line of it with his eyes, craning his neck so he can see where it circles the interior of their home. "What is it?"

"Watch," she orders, vibrating with excitement. He tries to pull her into his lap, but she shakes her head with a big grin.

"Why can't I hold you while I wait?" he pouts, and she laughs.

"In a minute," she promises and then gives a little squeal of delight when the first tram car appears from the small tunnel that she built for it under the bed.

"That's brilliant," Selon exclaims and plucks the tram from the track to examine it more closely. "You have every detail here. There is even a little person inside."

"Does the little person inside look familiar?" she asks with a grin. Selon's brow furrows, and he gives her a quizzical look.

He hazards a guess. "To my untrained eye, it looks like a Hissa male."

"You would be right. That one's you," she bursts out as if she's been holding in those words. "Put it back on the tracks. There's another one coming," she orders. He sets the tram carefully back on the tracks, grinning when it starts trundling off.

"How did you do that?" he asks in wonder. "The detail is amazing. And you haven't asked me to get you anything, so I'm assuming this was all made from the boxes of parts you brought home."

"All of it," she confirms proudly.

"You're a genius," he tells her sincerely, and she flushes with pleasure. She's about to deny it when the next tram appears.

"Grab it," she demands, so he plucks it up and looks inside.

"Oh, this one's easy, that's you. What did you make the black hair out of?"

"Wire insulation," she answers.

"Is that a teeny-tiny toolbelt around your waist?" he asks, putting his eye right up to the tram window.

"I had to give myself a miniature toolbelt so I wouldn't be confused with Mara," she explains.

"Logical," Selon agrees with a smile and sets the tram down on the track and watches it start moving away. "We need to let others see this. It's decorative and brilliant. The Council might want to display it somewhere."

Ignoring his words, she points down at the track, "There's one more tram."

"Let me guess. Your sister is in this one. Does she have Tiran wrapped around her waist instead of a tool belt?" he asks as he picks up the tram, bringing it up to eye level. She's silent, waiting for him to understand what he's seeing.

"I'm not sure what this is—" he starts. She watches the scale pattern on his head go pale. He grips the tram to his chest and looks up at her, his eyes wide with shock and hope.

"It's—" he starts and has to swallow. She crawls into his lap, prying the tram from his fingers and setting it aside.

"Yes, my love," she whispers in his ear, wrapping her arms around his neck and holding him tight. "It's a baby in the last tram. Our baby."

He draws her away from him so he can look her in the face and then down at her belly. "My young is in there?"

"I went to medical to see Mender Dimon today. He confirmed it and promised to keep it quiet until tomorrow," she explains. He reaches down to stroke her belly with a gentle, shaking hand.

"I never imagined I could be any happier," he confesses. "When you were so brave and stood in front of the Council for me. I never thought I could feel more joy than when you chose me."

Her breath hitches. "And now?"

When he meets her eyes, she sees nothing but love shining back at her. "You tell me I'm your strength, but you're the one who saved me," he tells her simply. "And this child will know nothing but love. Our child will be cherished and adored. You've single-handedly given Hissa a future."

"I thought that started with Mara," she argues with a little shake of her head. "Or maybe Mian. But not me."

"No, my love, they gave us hope." He kisses her gently on the lips. "You've given us a tomorrow we didn't think we would ever have."

She tries to blink back tears, but she can't. "I love you so much."

"My brave little *shamira*, it can't possibly be as much as I love you." He wipes away her tears and draws her closer. "I know you're used to me being calm, but I might not be so collected once our young joins us."

"Don't worry," she says with a soft laugh. "I know a couple of great places you can hide if everything gets to be too much for you."

"Only if you join me in these hiding spots," he whispers.

"Always," she promises.

Neither one notices the three trams on their miniature tracks are no longer separated. Now they're gently touching front to back as they trundle around the room.

Dear Readers,

Thank you for reading *Tempting Selon*. If you want more Hissa Warrior the next book, *Defying Kilan* is available to read. Be patient with Deena and Kilan. They were hard to write because they tended to want to fight, but they're story ended up being so sweet they brought me to tears!

I hope you enjoyed *Tempting Selon* enough to leave a review! As an indie writer without the support of a publishing company, I need all the help I can get. Your good reviews keep me writing.

If you have any questions, comments, or suggestions feel free to contact me via email: author@rk-munin.com

Check out my website, it's got all the links and free novellas for signing up for my newsletter:
www.RK-Munin.com

Here's a QR code for easy access:

Cheers,
Rye

OTHER BOOKS BY RK MUNIN

-Science Fiction-

Hissa Warrior Series
Rescuing Halin (Mian and Halin)
Buying Tiran (Mara and Tiran)
Tempting Selon (Lara and Selon)
Defying Kilan (Deena and Kilan)
Healing Mavito (Raleen and Mavito)
Claiming Yopin (Mouse and Yopin)
Teasing Woken (Safena and Woken)
Defending Revin (Kamaril and Revin) – Coming soon

Human Pets of Talin Series
Loving Captivity (Sora and Searin)
Escaping Captivity (Lakin and Dalt)
Negotiating Captivity (Nalia and Derani)
Fighting Captivity (Zia and Palforma)
Tender Captivity (Jinna and Holian - This is a novella you
can get for free by signing up for my newsletter)
Craving Captivity (Lasha and Tamerin)
The Twelve Nights of Halloheen: A holiday mashup novella
(Isla and Tisuran)
Stealing Captivity – Coming soon

Origins (A Human Pets of Talin Series)
Creating Captivity (Ari and Bazium)
Gossamer Chains (Rain and Hesarium)
Golden Cages – Coming soon

-Paranormal /Urban Fantasy-

Ours Evermore Series
Two Wolves for Soren (Soren, Kalli, and Quinn)
A Hacker, Vampire, and Chimera Walk into a Bar….(Tobias,
Briar, and Memphis)
When Darkness Meets Dawn (Imani, Lex, and Mac)
Tag, You're It (Short Story)

Kidnapping Their Third (Cora, Pike, and Kimble) – Coming soon

Pastries on a Plate and Blood in a Mug (Novella) – Coming soon

Alpha Series

Alpha Mage (Emma and Kade)

His Alpha Mage (Avery and Jason – Novella)

Alpha King (Cathleen and Lazlo)

New Clan Series

Stray Wolf (Steph and Eli)

Lost Lion (Maeve and Cyrus)

Reluctant Cervid (Tavi and Donovan)

Broken Thorn (Sabina and Theodosius)

9 781962 699075